BRENDA

AT THE PROM

Other Books by Jack Weyland

BRENDA

AT THE PROM

JACK WEYLAND

Deseret Book Company
Salt Lake City, Utah

No part of this book may be reproduced in any
form or by any means without permission in writing
from the publisher, Deseret Book Company,
P.O. Box 30178, Salt Lake City, Utah 84130.
Deseret Book is a registered trademark of
Deseret Book Company.

First printing August 1988
Second printing October 1988

Library of Congress Cataloging-in-Publication Data

Weyland, Jack, 1940–
    Brenda at the prom / Jack Weyland
        p.   cm.
    ISBN 0-87579-150-6 : $9.95 (est.)
    I. Title.
PS3573.E99B74   1988
813'.54 — dc19   88-14880
                                          CIP

Kade began each day of his freshman year in high school waiting for Brenda to take him to early-morning seminary. They lived about fifteen miles from the small farming community of Shelby, Montana.

Even though Kade's family lived in a farmhouse, they weren't farmers. His father, Paul Ellis, worked for a regional bank whose headquarters were in Chicago. They had moved from Illinois just that summer and were renting a farmhouse from the agri-corporation that had bought the farm after the owner went bankrupt.

Brenda Sloan was two years older than Kade, a junior in high school. On the first day of school, as she pulled in front of the house, Kade grabbed his school supplies, ran out to her battered yellow pickup, and climbed in. "Hi," he called out cheerfully. "Nice day, isn't it?"

"I suppose," she said, making it sound like "I spose."

Kade got in and looked around. A beat-up radio, missing a plastic knob, blared out a country-western song. A horse blanket was draped over the seat to cover the rips in the black vinyl upholstery. He tried to shut the door on his side, but the lock wouldn't catch.

"You have to really slam it," she said.

He tried it again. Still no luck.

"Put some muscle into it."

He pulled as hard as he could, but it still wouldn't lock.

"Here, let me do it." She reached over him and slammed the door with a mighty thud. This time it stayed shut.

Brenda shifted into first gear and let out the clutch. Nothing happened. She grabbed a hammer from under the seat, stepped outside, crawled underneath the frame, hit something, then got back in again. "Linkage," she said.

"You fixed it?"

"Yeah, for now."

Kade was impressed—he'd never fixed anything in his life.

As they traveled along the graveled county road, he studied her features. She had a very straight, but not too long, nose, dark bushy eyebrows, full lips, and a long neck, which made her sandy-brown hair seem shorter than it actually was. She wore a faded Levi jacket and jeans. From where he sat he couldn't tell the color of her eyes, but from having seen her in church, he knew they were a muted green.

"Thanks for agreeing to take me to seminary," he said.

She shrugged. "It's no big deal. Besides, your dad offered to help pay for the gas. I sure wasn't about to turn that down. Money's hard enough to come by these days."

"I'm kind of nervous," he said, "this being my first day at school and all."

"I s'pose," she said, not very interested in his problems.

He sighed. "I wish I was wearing contact lenses today instead of these dumb glasses. I've almost got enough money saved for them. My parents can't understand why I want 'em though. They say I look okay with glasses." He removed his glasses. "I think I look better this way, don't you?"

The song on the radio had put her in another world. She glanced over at him. "What?"

He put his glasses back on. "Never mind, it wasn't important. I don't usually talk this much. I guess I'm kinda hyper today. I just don't know what to expect in school. You're about the only one I'll know." He paused. "Any chance I could eat lunch with you?"

"Forget it. I don't want some little ninth grader tagging after me."

"Oh."

She looked over at him. "Look, it's nothing personal. You'll feel the same way when you're my age."

"But you're the only one I know. If you could just let me eat at your table until I get to know someone else . . . just for one day even."

"I said no, didn't I?"

"Yes."

"Then just drop it, okay?"

"Okay."

"Good. Now just be quiet and listen to the radio."

"How about turning to another station?" he asked.

"What for?"

"I don't like cowboy music."

"Then plug your ears."

He didn't talk the rest of the way into town.

Seminary was held at the home of the teacher, Sister Simmons, with Kade and Brenda and Sister Simmons's daughter Melissa, who was a year younger than Brenda. This year they would be studying the Old Testament.

After seminary the two girls and Kade went out to the pickup.

"Melissa, you want to ride shotgun?" Brenda asked.

"Sure." Melissa turned to Kade as if she expected

him to do something. "I'm riding shotgun," she said to him.

He was still confused. "What does that mean?"

"Where you from, anyway?"

"Illinois."

"It figures. Get in. You're riding in the middle."

On the way to school, they treated him as if he weren't even there except for the fact that every time Brenda had to shift gears, he had to move his legs to get out of her way.

When they reached the school parking lot, Brenda turned to Kade. "I'm leaving at three o'clock sharp. If you're not here then, I'll go without you."

"I'll be here."

Kade went to the principal's office. A woman helped him fill out the necessary forms. By the time he finished, it was nearly ten.

The first class he made it to was gym. The class didn't have to suit up the first day. They were all sitting around on bleachers in the gym when the gym teacher, Coach Brannigan, who was also the football coach, walked in. "All right, girls, pipe down," he called out.

Kade hated it when a man called a group of boys "girls."

After taking roll, the coach went over class rules with them, peppering his comments with stories about boys who'd messed up in past years. Near the end of the period, he went to a thick manila rope hanging from the ceiling. "If any of you want more than a C out of this course, you'll have to climb this to the ceiling and lower yourself back down again. Any of you think you're man enough to do that?"

Several boys raised their hands. Kade looked at how high the ceiling was and decided to settle for a C.

After class Kade went up to Coach Brannigan. "Do you happen to know if there's a soccer league in town?"

The coach smirked. "The girls' gym classes play soccer. Maybe you ought to see if they'll let you join 'em."

Kade was sorry he'd asked. Marvin Mudlin, a large boy with huge arms and shoulders, had overheard. "I bet they'd let him play too, wouldn't they, coach?"

Kade turned to leave.

"Ellis," the coach called out.

Kade turned around. "What?"

"Why did you ask about soccer anyway?"

"I used to play on a team before we moved here."

"Where are you from?"

"Illinois."

"You're in Montana now. This is football country. There's no soccer here."

"Except for girls. Right, coach?" Marvin Mudlin smirked.

What a bunch of jerks, Kade thought as he made his way to his next class.

At three o'clock, he hurried to his locker, then went outside. Brenda's pickup was easy to spot in the parking lot. It had once been yellow, but since then the worst rust spots had been primed with a rust inhibitor, creating a patchwork hodgepodge of browns and yellows. Brenda showed up and they left for home. A short section of pipe in the bed of the pickup rolled back and forth everytime they started or stopped.

Brenda listened to cowboy songs all the way home and didn't even ask him how school had gone.

Every school day began with an early morning ride to town and ended with an afternoon ride back home. Because of the difference in their ages, Brenda didn't talk to him much, which meant he had nearly an hour a day to be with a girl who treated him as if he weren't even there. Even if he stared directly at her, it didn't seem to faze her.

Kade wasn't sure how it began, but he soon found himself fascinated with her face. Because she didn't use much makeup, she sometimes seemed plain, but in the morning as they traveled east toward town, the sun would often catch the highlights in her hair. The interplay between light and shadow accentuated her high cheekbones. For an instant she became more beautiful than any girl he'd ever seen.

Kade's room on the second floor of the farmhouse his family lived in had been converted from the attic by the original owners. The room was long and narrow, with sloping walls matching the roofline on two sides and a small window at each end. The room had a hardwood floor, with a throw-rug next to his bed so he wouldn't freeze his feet when he got up in the morning. To heat the room, the original owner had cut a hole in the floor big enough for a heating vent. Kade found that if he sat near the vent, he could sometimes hear what was being said downstairs.

One day after school, he sat at the desk in his room and began drawing a picture of Brenda. It was a straight front view that focused on her eyes. For some strange reason, perhaps because her distinctive eyebrows made her seem strong-willed and aloof, he turned her into a storybook princess. A veil covered her hair completely, creating a sense of mystery. Perhaps she was traveling at night through dark cobblestoned streets and needed the veil to hide her identity. And yet her very gaze, bold and uncompromising, would give her away as nobility to anyone who looked at her closely enough.

When he finished the sketch, he was fascinated with what he had created. After that he drew pictures of Brenda nearly every day.

Sometimes when Kade was drawing in his room upstairs, he could hear his mother in the living room below, practicing her violin. He had grown up listening to her play the violin. In Illinois, she had been in a symphony orchestra, but there wasn't one in Shelby.

Kade found that it wasn't just Brenda that inspired the artist in him. It was also the area where he was living, just sixty miles east of Glacier Park. Each day on his way home he saw the snowcapped mountains, while in the fields nearby was the brown and tan stubble left after the harvest, as well as the tender green shoots of winter wheat that depended on the snow to come like a blanket and protect it from the bitter winds that would soon come roaring down from Canada. Sometimes he wondered if anyone else saw the world the way he did. And if they did, how could they stand it? How could people live near those mountains and stop looking at them long enough to get any work done? It was all so magnificent.

Before long Kade needed a place to hide the growing stack of drawings. He went to his closet and pulled down from a shelf the box for his Monopoly game. He set the drawings in the box and returned the box to the closet.

As the days passed, he felt himself slipping deeper into another world, a place within himself where things could be created and brought to life. Sometimes he had to fight to come out of that world long enough to do his homework. So far Kade's parents were unaware that much of the time he spent in his room was taken up drawing pictures of Brenda. They assumed he was studying. He felt certain his father wouldn't approve. To Kade, his father was a well-oiled machine, someone who went to work each day in a three-piece suit, came home at night and asked how school was going, discussed finances and bills and budgets with his wife, settled in his favorite chair after dinner and read the *Wall Street Journal* until time for TV news, then went to bed.

Sometimes at night his father worked at his computer. Once he showed Kade a spread-sheet software package he had just purchased, which allowed a person to create endless rows and columns of numbers. "This might be useful to you someday," he had said. Kade felt certain that would never happen because even if you could fill all the rows and columns with numbers, what had you gained? They were still just numbers.

Kade wondered what his parents would say if they found the sketches of Brenda. They might think he was in love with her. But that wasn't it at all. What he loved were the images he created of her. As time went on, he found himself increasingly in awe of the creative process itself. Somewhere inside him was a reservoir that never ran dry.

Each day along the gravel road, he studied Brenda. Sometimes she seemed lonely, almost sullen, but at other times, especially after she got used to having him around, she sang along with the radio to her favorite western songs. And he, mostly ignored by her, sat and watched and listened.

And when he got home he drew.

One day in gym, the boys suited up and played touch football outside. After class, as Kade was coming out of the shower, someone snapped him from behind with a towel. He turned around to see Marvin Mudlin standing there holding one end of a wet towel.

"Knock it off," Kade complained.

Marvin smirked and snapped the towel at him again. Kade jumped back to avoid being hit.

"I mean it."

"Hey, what're you gonna do if I don't stop?"

Kade knew that to fight Marvin would be suicide. "I'll tell the coach."

"What's the matter? Can't you fight your own battles?" Marvin flicked the towel at him again, catching him just above the kneecap.

"I said knock it off!"

The coach came into the room. "What's going on?"

"Nothing," Marvin said. "We were just having some fun."

"You two get dressed and quit horsing around."

Kade went to his locker and put his clothes on as fast as he could.

That afternoon on the way home Kade waited until they were out of town before reaching over and clicking off Brenda's radio.

"Hey, leave it where it was."

"I need to talk to you," he said.

"What for?"

"I just do. Look, it's not going to kill you to talk to me, is it? We're out here where nobody can see us, in case you're worried someone might find out you actually broke down and talked to me."

She raised her eyebrows. "What's got into you anyway?"

"Do girls ever snap each other with towels in the locker room after a shower?"

She shook her head. "You are really weird."

"Guys do sometimes."

"Kade, I don't really care what happens in the boys' locker room, okay?"

"Today a guy snapped me with a towel."

"So?"

"What do you think I should've done?"

She shrugged. "I don't know—snapped him back, I guess."

"It was Marvin Mudlin. He must outweigh me by a hundred pounds."

"You can't let people walk all over you. Sometimes you've got to fight for your rights."

"If I'd have fought him, he would've killed me."

"He might've hit you a couple of times, but he'd

never mess with you again because he'd know you'd always fight back."

He paused. "I've never fought anybody in my whole life."

"Why not?"

"My parents say it's not right to fight."

"Sure, that's easy for them to say—nobody's snapping them with a towel whenever they get out of a shower. Look, Kade, if you don't fight back, Marvin's going to keep hassling you. So make up your mind." Having given him the benefit of her advice, she turned the radio back on.

That night Kade came up with his own plan: he wouldn't take showers after gym anymore. While everyone else was showering, he would hurry up and get dressed and be gone before Marvin could get to him.

He tried it the next time he had gym, and it worked fine. However, on the way home Brenda rolled down her window. "Good grief, Kade, is that you?"

"What?"

"Something in here smells real bad. You got a problem?"

He blushed. "Maybe so. I didn't take a shower after gym today."

She shook her head. "Kade, you can't let people push you around."

"Nobody pushed me around today."

"Sure, that's because you turned tail and ran."

"I didn't run. I just didn't take a shower, that's all."

"And so after gym you went to all your classes smelling like that?"

"It's not that bad."

"Not that bad? How can you say that? You smell like something that's been dead for two weeks."

"I couldn't think of anything else to do about Marvin."

"You have to learn to stand up for yourself. Fight him if you have to."

"I don't know how to fight."

"You can learn."

"How? There's not even a YMCA in this dumb town."

"What do you need a YMCA for?"

"To take boxing lessons."

"I can't believe you said that. You don't need boxing lessons. Just start fighting. You'll pick it up fast enough."

"Sure, except by the time I learn I'll be dead. His arms are at least twice as big as mine. Forget it. I'm not fighting him."

"What if you wait until he turns his back to you and then you hit him from behind and tackle him?"

"This happens right after we've taken a shower."

"So?"

"So we don't have any clothes on."

"I understand showers, okay? So what's the problem?"

"I don't want to be wrestling some guy when neither one of us is dressed."

"Have you got a plan?"

"Yeah, sort of."

"What is it?"

"I was thinking of maybe putting poison ivy on his soap so he'll get this really bad rash and have to be out of school for a long time."

She shook her head. "You're hopeless."

It was mainly because of wanting Brenda's approval that Kade finally decided to fight Marvin. After the next gym class, as he was drying himself off by his locker, Marvin came and snapped him again with a towel. When he turned to walk away, Kade lunged at him. Because the floor was slick, Marvin fell down and hit his head on one of the benches. At first Kade worried he'd killed Marvin, but then Marvin slowly sat up, gingerly touched his head with his hand, and got up. The other boys gathered around, eager to see a fight.

"You'll pay for this," Marvin threatened.

Marvin shoved Kade backwards against the lockers and then hit him twice in the face and once in the stomach. Kade doubled over and fell to the floor, gasping for breath.

Marvin loomed over him. "Get up, you little twerp. I'm not done with you yet."

Kade was not about to get up just so he could be knocked down again.

"I'll get you up myself then." Marvin grabbed Kade by the shoulders and hoisted him up and slammed him against a locker. When Kade saw the look on Marvin's face, he knew he'd better do something. He ducked just before the blow got to him, and Marvin's fist hit the locker. It sounded like a gun going off, and he cried out in pain.

The noise brought Coach Brannigan in from the gym. "You two! In my office!"

Once they were in his office, the coach shut the door, then turned to face them. "What's going on here?"

"He kept snapping me with a towel," Kade said. "I told him to lay off, but he wouldn't, so I decided to do something about it."

"Yeah, the little twerp came from behind and knocked me down," Marvin added.

The coach turned to Marvin. "Are you okay?"

"Well, I guess so," Marvin said. "I hit my head against the bench when I fell down, and then later he ducked a punch, and my hand hit the lockers."

"Here, let me take a look." The coach carefully examined Marvin's injuries. "I think you'll be okay by Friday."

"Hey, what's the deal here?" Kade complained. "This ape nearly kills me and you're worrying he might've hurt his precious hand." Suddenly the light dawned. "Oh, I get it. King Kong here is on the football team, right?"

"What of it?" Marvin shot back.

"I should've known. It's the same wherever you go. You look for the biggest jerks in school and they're always on the football team." He turned to the coach. "You're not even going to punish him, are you? Of course not. Football players always get special treatment, don't they? Well, that stinks, if you ask me. It's not fair."

"Not fair?" the coach raged. "Not fair? I'll tell you what's not fair!" He went into a long tirade about trying to field a football team with not enough funds, equipment, and personnel. He ended up facing off at Kade. "You report to my office after school."

"I can't."

"What do you mean, you can't?"

"I live out of town, and my ride goes home right after school."

"When I tell someone to report after school, I expect them to do it and not give me a bunch of flimsy excuses why they can't."

"If I stay, how am I going to get home?" Kade knew his father would probably give him a ride home, but he didn't want to mention that to the coach. He wanted to go with Brenda so he could tell her about the fight.

The coach paused long enough to cool down. "Do you have a free period tomorrow?"

"Yeah, at eleven o'clock."

"Report to my office then. Understood?"

"What about him?" Kade asked, glancing at Marvin. "When's he reporting to you?"

"Mudlin, I want you here too," the coach ordered.

"Me? Why me? I didn't do anything."

"You started it," Kade shot back.

"I did not."

"You two—get out of here!" the coach roared.

As the day progressed, Kade looked worse. He had two black-and-blue bruises on his face. He also had a headache and had to go to the office and ask for a couple of aspirin.

Strangely enough, though, fighting Marvin had made him a celebrity. In English class, Whitney Lindquist, the best-looking freshman girl in school, came up to him. "Weren't you scared of fighting Marvin? He's so big."

"Not so big he can't be knocked off his perch," Kade said, trying to sound as macho as possible.

Whitney was standing closer to him than any girl had ever done before. He realized he was breathing some of the very air she was exhaling. "I'm glad somebody finally stood up to him," she said. "He used to pick on my cousin all the time."

"If he ever bothers your cousin again, just let me know. I'll take care of him for you."

"Thanks. Well, I'll be seeing you." She paused. "Kade, if you want to call me tonight, it'd be okay."

He couldn't believe his ears but tried to be nonchalant about it. "Well, yeah, I might call you—if I'm not too busy, that is."

After school Kade got to the pickup before Brenda. It was unlocked, so he climbed in and waited. When she came, she took one look at his face. "Gosh, Kade, you okay?"

"Yeah, I'm all right. I fought Marvin, just the way we talked about. I tackled him from behind when he wasn't looking. Then he got up and hit me. He hurt his fist real bad when I ducked a punch and he hit the lockers, and then the coach came in and stopped the whole thing."

"All right, Kade! You showed him! Are you glad you did it?"

"Yeah, I am. It was great afterwards. Whitney Lundquist came up and talked to me. She's glad I fought

Marvin because he used to pick on her cousin. You should've seen her. I'm not kidding—she was practically hanging all over me. She pretty much begged me to call her up tonight."

Brenda smiled. "So, do you like being a hero to all the little ninth-grade girls?"

He grinned. "Sure, why not?" He paused. "Thanks for telling me what to do."

It was no surprise that his parents didn't approve of his fighting Marvin. They said there are other ways to settle a dispute. But Kade knew that none of their ways would have resulted in Whitney Lundquist coming up and asking him to phone her. He decided the next time he had a problem, he would go to Brenda for advice.

That night, because he wanted privacy, he took the phone into the bathroom, shut the door, and dialed Whitney's number. She answered.

"Whitney, this is Kade."

"Oh, hi. How are you doing?"

"Okay. Of course, my folks got mad at me for fighting." He paused. "But sometimes a guy has to do what a guy has to do."

"I know. Kade, are you going with anyone?"

"No."

"Would you like to go with me?"

Kade paused. He wasn't even supposed to date until he was sixteen. But, hey, no use worrying about technicalities at a time like this. "Sure, why not?"

"Okay. Are you going to the dance Friday night?"

"I suppose."

"Would you like to take me?"

"Yeah, might as well—since we're going together. I'll meet you there."

"Aren't you going to pick me up?"

"You mean, like in a car?"

"Yes, of course."

"I don't have a driver's license."

"You don't?" she said. "I do."

"You do?" His voice cracked as he said it.

"Sure. In Montana you can get a permit to drive when you turn fourteen."

"In Illinois you have to be sixteen."

"You're not in Illinois anymore, Kade."

"I asked my parents about it when we moved here, and they said they wanted me to wait until I at least turned fifteen."

"Are you saying you don't even know how to drive?" she asked.

He tried to get back his fading confidence. "Well, no, but how hard can it be?"

"I guess maybe the guys I usually go out with are older than you."

He cleared his throat. "You've dated other guys?"

"Sure. Last summer I dated a college student."

Kade gulped. "But you're only fourteen, aren't you?"

"I'm almost fifteen. Besides, I'm very mature for my age."

"Some people I know don't actually start dating until they're sixteen."

"Why would anyone want to wait that long?" she asked.

"I'm just telling you what some people do, that's all."

"If you can't drive, I guess I could meet you at the dance. What do you want to do after the dance?"

"I don't know. Go home, I guess."

"I know where there's a party we can go to. Are you a party animal?" she asked.

"Well, sure, I guess so. I've been to parties."

"I'm talking about parties where everyone gets wasted."

"Wasted?" His voice cracked as he said it.

"One time I was so out of it that when I woke up the next morning I couldn't remember where I was or anything that happened the night before. Has that ever happened to you?"

There was a long silence. "No, but sometimes I can't remember where I put things."

"Kade, tell me the truth, have you ever got drunk?"

"Well, no, not actually."

"Have you ever even tried it?"

"No."

"Why not?"

"I just never wanted to."

"You ought to try it at least once. How can you be sure you don't like it unless you try it?"

It didn't seem fair. This was his one chance to go with the best-looking girl his age in school. He had purposely avoided mentioning the Church just so she'd accept him, but it wasn't working out the way he wanted.

"You want me to help you get started, Kade?" she asked.

This was a big decision—he was afraid it would cost him Whitney's friendship. He sighed. "I guess not. Thanks anyway, though."

"How come you won't even try it?"

There was no escaping. "The reason I don't drink is because that's what my church teaches."

There was a long pause. "You belong to a church?"

"Yeah."

"And you go to church every Sunday?"

"Yeah."

"Gosh, Kade, that's nice and all, but the thing is, I guess I'm looking for a guy who's more of a real man."

To Kade this was the ultimate insult.

"I think we'd better hang up," she said. "My mom needs to use the phone."

"Are we still going together?" he asked.

"I don't think so. Look, I'll see you around, okay?"

"Yeah, okay. 'Bye." Kade hung up the phone and came out of the bathroom.

"Kade," his mother called, "be sure and put your dirty clothes in the hamper tonight before you go to bed."

"I wish everyone would quit treating me like a little kid," he grumbled before stomping up the stairs to his room.

"What does a guy have to do to become a real man?" Kade asked Brenda when she picked him up the next morning.

"How should I know? Ask your dad."

"He'd tell me not to worry about it."

"Why are you worrying about it?"

"Whitney broke up with me last night."

"I didn't know you were even going with her."

"We were for about three minutes. Then she broke up because she said I wasn't man enough for her."

"Kade, you're fourteen, right? You're not supposed to be a man at fourteen."

"I just wish people would quit treating me like a little kid."

"The fact is, to someone my age, you *are* a little kid. There's probably nothing you can do about it. Look, if you want to know the truth, being sixteen is no picnic either." She paused. "I don't have any real close friends in school."

"What about Melissa?"

"She's okay, I guess, but she and I are a lot different. And sometimes she really gets on my nerves." She sighed. "Most everybody my age parties every weekend."

"Whitney wanted me to go drinking with her but I said no. That's why she broke up with me."

"Drinking is a dumb thing to do."

"I know, but still, I wish I hadn't lost her."

She shrugged. "That's life." And with that she turned on the radio.

"Why do we always have to listen to cowboy songs?" he complained.

"Simple—because it's my rig."

At eleven o'clock Kade reported to Coach Brannigan. "The way I figure it," the coach said, "you've got two hours of detention coming for what you did yesterday. You can either sit in a chair or you can make yourself useful. What'll it be?"

"I'd rather do something than just sit around."

The coach led him into a room containing a large washing machine and a clothes dryer—and a huge stack of dirty uniforms. He told Kade exactly what to do. "You got that?"

"I think so."

"Good. I've got a class now, but I'll come back when I can to see how you're doing."

"Who usually does this?" Kade asked.

"We had a student equipment manager, but last week he up and quit on me. I guess it wasn't glamorous enough for him. I've been doing it myself until I can find someone else to help out."

"You shouldn't have to do this."

"Tell me about it." With that, the coach left.

Kade enjoyed the challenge of doing the laundry exactly the way the coach had told him. He separated everything into three piles, each waiting its turn to be thrown into the washing machine.

He was sitting at the folding table reading a magazine for high school coaches when Marvin walked in the room. "How's it going?" he said.

Kade was wary, even though Marvin seemed friendly. "Okay."

"Looks like the coach put you to work, huh?"

"Yeah."

"I just talked to him. He told me to come in here and help out."

"There's not much to do right now."

"Is it all right if I stick around?" Marvin asked.

"I guess so."

"You're kind of a spunky kid, aren't you."

"Not usually."

"You were yesterday, that's for sure."

"I don't like to be pushed around."

"I understand. Hey, I was way out of line. My dad got really mad when he found out what I'd been doing. He said I could've done some permanent damage to you." He paused. "I didn't, did I?"

"No."

"Good. He said I had to come and apologize."

"Oh."

It was an awkward moment. They stared at each other. "Well, I guess that's taken care of," Marvin said.

"I guess so."

"How come you don't mind washing our sweaty outfits?"

Kade shrugged. "It's no big deal."

"Maybe you should become the equipment manager."

"What would I have to do?"

"Well, keep up with the wash. And during a game you'd be in charge of giving players water and making sure the first-aid kit is on the field. That's about it. Why don't you talk to the coach about it?"

"Maybe I will."

"Tell me something," Marvin said. "Is it hard moving to a new town?"

"Yeah, it kinda is."

"My dad says if things don't get better, we'll have to move to where he can make a decent living. I'd hate to leave here though. Look, I'm sorry for giving you a hard time. I'll say one thing for you, you've got a lot of nerve for someone so small."

"I'm not small. I looked it up in a book. I'm average for my age." He paused. "Maybe you're just extra big. You ever think about that?"

"I'm older than most guys in the ninth grade. I was held back a year."

"Oh."

"Not because I'm dumb though. I just got sick, that's all."

"Why did you decide to pick on me?"

"I don't know. You just looked like someone it'd be fun to pick on."

"Was it because of my glasses?"

"I don't think so. Why?"

"I hate 'em. As soon as I can, I'm going to get me a pair of contacts."

"I've got a cousin who wears contacts. She likes them a lot. She got 'em in Great Falls. Got a really good buy, too. I'll see if I can get the name of the place."

"That'd be good. I'm not ready to get 'em right now because I still have to save up a little more money. My parents won't help me out any. They say I look good enough with glasses. I don't care though. I'm getting 'em anyway."

"How come you want contacts? To impress the girls?" Marvin teased.

"Not really."

"I bet that's the reason, all right."

"No way."

"Have you ever gone with a girl?"

"No."

"You didn't have one in Illinois?"

"No."

"Have you got yourself one picked out here yet?"

"I thought I'd just play the field for a while."

Marvin laughed. "That means you can't find anyone either, right?"

"Right."

"Me neither." He looked at the clock. "Well, I guess I should go."

"Yeah, sure. See you in gym class."

"Don't worry about being hassled anymore. And if anyone ever gives you a hard time, just let me know, okay?"

"Yeah, thanks."

"No problem. Well, see you around." Marvin left.

The washing machine stopped, and Kade made the transfer of clothes into the dryer. He picked up the next pile and dumped it into the washing machine, then started both machines and sat down.

The coach came in. "Looks like you're doing a real fine job."

To receive praise from the coach made Kade feel good. "If you want, I can help out all the time."

"You mean be my equipment manager?"

"Yeah." He paused. "There's just one problem—would I have to stay after school?"

"Well, we could use you after school, but I know you've got to catch your ride home. I think we can pretty much take care of things during the practices if you can keep caught up on the laundry, and, of course, we'd need you for the games. Most of 'em are on Friday night."

"That's no problem. I could come every day during this period and wash the things from the night before."

"That'd be great. There's funguses that grow in sweaty clothes that can make an athlete's life miserable. So what you'll be doing to keep things clean is very important to the team."

"I'd like to do it."

"Well, how about that? You've made my day, I'll tell

you." He looked at the clock on the wall. "I guess I'd better get to my next class."

As Kade worked, he realized he was whistling one of the cowboy songs he'd heard that morning in Brenda's pickup.

After school Kade could hardly wait to tell Brenda. "Guess what? I'm going to be helping out the football team."

"You mean you're on the team?"

"Not exactly. I'm going to be the equipment manager."

"What does the equipment manager do?"

Kade hesitated. "He takes care of the equipment."

"Yeah, sure, but what exactly do you do?"

He paused. "I wash towels and dirty uniforms." He watched for her reaction. He hoped she wouldn't make fun of him.

"Oh," she said. "Well, that's nice, Kade."

"It's also important. The coach told me that if they don't have clean uniforms, they could get this really bad fungus. If they got that, it'd be pretty bad. They'd all be standing around scratching themselves instead of concentrating on the game."

"That'd be awful, not only for the team but also for the people who come to watch. What else does an equipment manager do?"

"I'm responsible for the first-aid kit."

"That's important."

"And I make sure they get water if they're thirsty."

"I'll bet they appreciate that. I know I would if I were a football player."

"So in a way, it's like I'm helping them win. And I get to stand around on the sidelines during a game. I think they might even let me buy a team jacket. And another thing, I'll get to know all the players. So if you or any of your friends ever want me to put in a good word to one of them, just let me know."

She smiled. "I can see you're an important guy to know."

That night after supper Kade told his parents.

"It sounds to me like just an excuse to get you to do their dirty work," his mother said.

"Not at all," his father said. "Every football team has to have people who can help. I think it'll be good for Kade. He'll be helping the team out, and he'll make new friends. Kade, if that's what you want to do, then I'd say go for it."

And so Kade became the new equipment manager for the team.

CHAPTER 2

The next day at work Paul Ellis got a phone call from Dwight Allen, a corporate vice-president of the bank in Chicago. Dwight had been the one who had asked Paul to move to Montana to run the Shelby bank.

"Paul, I was thinking about you this morning. How are things going out there in the Wild West?"

"Not too bad."

"How's Denise doing?"

"She's missed being in the symphony this year, but other than that, I'd say she's adjusting to life in a small town."

"Paul, look, something's come up that I need to talk to you about. When we first talked about you going to Montana, I mentioned we didn't anticipate that this'd be a long assignment. We've had our eyes on you for some time, and we've just been waiting for the time when we can put you in place as one of our regional managers. But with this farm crisis and the problems the manager you replaced created for us, we needed someone with your objectivity who could go in and set things right."

"I'm working on it."

"I'm sure you are. My main reason for calling is that an opening has come up a little sooner than we anticipated. One of our regional managers had a heart attack last night. To be honest, we don't think he's going to make it, and even if he does, I doubt he'll be able to return to work. So if you can wrap up what you've got to do in, say, about a month, then we could move you into our Indiana region. It would be a very good career move for you."

Paul was pleased. "Sounds good."

"Great. Of course, we'd like you to clear up things there in Shelby first."

"To tell you the truth, I don't enjoy very much being the bank's hatchet man."

"Nobody does, but sometimes it has to be done. So finish up so we can get you out of there soon. From what I've heard, you don't want to be there in the winter."

On Friday night Shelby High School had a home game. Kade stayed after school to prepare everything. His parents dutifully came to watch him perform as equipment manager.

One of the players loaned him a letter jacket so he'd look the part. It was too big for him, but he liked the way it made him feel to wear it.

When the players came off the field, he made sure there were towels to wipe the sweat off their faces and cups of water if they wanted some.

They lost 14 to 6, but Kade took consolation in the fact that the team, at least during the first quarter, looked clean.

The Mormon church was still struggling for survival in that part of Montana. There was a small branch in Shelby, which was part of the Great Falls Stake. The stake center was nearly a hundred miles away. Each Sunday Kade and his family went to church at the Odd Fellows Hall on Main Street, above the hardware store. They could usually count on about twenty people making it out to church on Sunday.

The branch had been in existence for five years, and for all that time the branch president had been Otis Cummings. On Saturday night President Mathesen, the stake president, phoned to ask Paul to meet him the next morning before church.

On Sunday President Mathesen asked Paul to serve as the next branch president. Paul said he wasn't sure how much longer he'd be in the area, but President Mathesen asked him to take the assignment for however long it was. Paul accepted the calling, and they talked about possible counselors. The list of candidates was not long. Brother Arnold, who had been the branch clerk since the branch was organized, said that was job enough for any man, and he didn't want anything else to do. Brother Aldrich, who was in his late sixties and had a hearing loss, refused any church callings that required talking to people. Sister Simmons's husband was not a member, and Brenda's father, although a member, seldom attended.

"Someone may turn up later," President Mathesen said.

After church Paul was set apart.

Kade soon learned what it meant to have his father serving as branch president. It meant the family went to church early, gathered up smelly ashtrays and empty beer bottles left there from the night before, opened the windows to air out the place, and set up folding chairs. Kade was the only active Aaronic Priesthood holder in the branch, so he set up and passed the sacrament every week.

After church Kade helped put the chairs back again. Then he and his mother usually went home while his dad and Brother Arnold counted donations and made out a deposit slip.

Paul's main goal as branch president was to find a replacement for himself when he left. He visited almost every family that first week and tried to encourage everyone to start coming out to church. He often wondered what would happen to the branch after he left. It appeared there was nobody else who could step in as branch president.

Once a month the early-morning seminary students from the small branches and wards in the stake met for a Super Saturday, which consisted of a seminary lesson taught by the seminary coordinator for the region, followed by an activity.

The first Super Saturday for the school year was held the next Saturday. Kade and Brenda rode to the stake center with Sister Simmons and Melissa. Brenda and Melissa sat in back and for the most part carried on their own private conversation, leaving Sister Simmons and Kade trying to think of what to say to each other.

"Kade, what's exciting in your life these days?" Sister Simmons asked.

"I'm the equipment manager for the football team."

"That's wonderful."

"It sounds wonderful until you find out what he does," Melissa said. "He washes the team's sweats. Big deal."

"I'll be able to get a letter jacket out of it."

Melissa giggled. "So when someone asks you what you lettered in, what are you going to tell them? Laundry?"

"Melissa," her mother said.

"Sorry, but it's so funny. Gosh, Kade, I wonder if there's an Olympic laundry team."

"Knock it off."

"Sorry. Gee whiz, you don't have to be so sensitive about everything."

A while later Sister Simmons asked what hobbies he had.

It was the first time he'd ever admitted it. "I like to draw."

"Are you taking an art class in school?"

"No."

"Do you draw very much?"

"Almost every day."

"What do you draw?"

Kade didn't want anyone to know that most of the pictures he drew were of Brenda. "Nothing much."

Brenda leaned forward. "I didn't know you liked art."

"I just got started in it."

"Sometime let me see what you've done," Brenda said.

"I'd like to see it too, Kade," Sister Simmons said.

"Sometime maybe."

"How about tomorrow after church?" Brenda asked.

"No. I don't want to show it to anyone yet."

"Well think about it, and when you're ready to let us see it, just let us know. Now there's donuts in a bag in the back seat, Melissa, if you want to get them out and pass them around. Oh, and there's orange juice too."

It took them two hours to get into the stake center in Great Falls, but it was worth it. For Kade it was fun to be with a large group of members his age. In Shelby the Church was so small that it was easy to believe he was the only guy in the world who didn't drink. That was all anyone in school talked about. Sometimes he felt as if he'd never fit in, no matter how hard he tried.

He met Linda Cooper, a girl his age, when they played volleyball in the gym after the lesson. She had short blond hair and a nice smile, and she liked to talk a lot, which was good for Kade because it put less pressure on him.

He also met lots of boys at Super Saturday. It was a comfort for him to be with them—some strong, some tall, some funny, some chubby, but all trying to live the way they'd been taught.

While he was playing volleyball, Kade saw Brenda walk out of the cultural hall with Jason Pasco. He wondered what that was all about.

After the activity, on their way out of town, Sister Simmons stopped at McDonald's. They went through the drive-through and ordered an early supper. It was her treat.

"Well, how was it today?" Sister Simmons asked as they cruised down I-15 for home.

"Brenda did okay for herself," Melissa teased. "She met Jason Pasco. *Oo la la!* Big time romance, hey, Brenda?"

"He's okay."

"Your mouth says okay but your eyes say wow," Melissa teased.

Brenda fought back a smile. "We just talked, that's all. It's no big deal."

"I saw the two of you standing in the hall, drooling over each other."

"Is Jason new?" Sister Simmons asked.

"Yes," Brenda said. "His family moved to Great Falls during the summer. His dad is the new superintendent of schools."

"What year is he in school?" Sister Simmons asked.

"He's a senior."

"What's he going to do after he graduates?"

"Marry Brenda," Melissa teased.

"He's going to work for a year and then go on a mission." Brenda paused. "He has a girl in the town where he came from. He's still interested in her."

"That won't last long, not with Brenda on the prowl."

"Melissa, I'm sure Brenda doesn't appreciate you talking like that," Sister Simmons said.

"All right, let's turn our attention to Kade then," Melissa said. "What a mover with the girls he's turned out to be."

"What are you talking about?" Kade said.

"Don't give me that. I saw you playing up to Linda Cooper."

"We were on the same team in volleyball. I was just talking strategy with her."

"I saw strategy out there all right, but it didn't have anything to do with volleyball. Did you know your voice dropped about an octave around her? And I noticed you took off your glasses. What for? So she could see your eyes? And that one time she got hit by the ball, there you were, giving her the big sympathy treatment. The way you were fussing over her, you'd think she'd been run over by a truck."

Surprisingly, Brenda took over where Melissa left off. "Look out, girls, 'cause Kade's hit town. And with his dark eyes and brown hair and sheepish grin, no heart is safe."

Kade denied Brenda's description of him, but he secretly wished it were true. It also made him wonder what it would be like if he and Brenda were the same age.

On the second Saturday in October the stake scheduled the first of a series of monthly stake youth dances in Great Falls. At first Sister Simmons was going to take the kids from Shelby in her car, but the night before she called to say she'd come down with a bad cold and wouldn't be able to go. And so it looked impossible for Kade and Brenda to go until Saturday afternoon, when

Brenda phoned and said she'd gotten permission to drive to the dance. If Kade was willing to share in the cost of the gas, he could go along with her. He quickly agreed.

Because of long travel from the outlying branches, the dance was scheduled to begin at seven and end at eleven. Brenda picked Kade up at five. She was wearing a dress. It was the only time he'd seen her in a dress except for Sundays. "You look nice," he said.

"I feel a little foolish, if you want to know the truth. Going to all this trouble for most likely nothing."

"You smell good too."

"My mom let me use some of her perfume. She's had it a long time but doesn't use it much anymore." She looked at Kade. "You look good too."

"It's no big deal."

"The weather report says it might snow tonight, so we'll have to be careful. This rig doesn't have much traction in the snow unless you put some weight in the back end, but then the gas mileage goes way down, so we try to hold off doing that until we absolutely have to. Money's real tight in our family this winter."

"How come?"

"Grasshoppers got a lot of our crop last year. You don't pay attention to things like that, do you?"

"Why should I? I'm not a farmer."

Thirty miles from Great Falls it started to snow and the wind picked up. It was a relief when they finally pulled into the parking lot at the stake center. They walked into the building together.

"I'm going to fix myself up before I go in," she said, "so I'll see you in there."

Kade wandered into the cultural hall and looked around. He walked over to one of the guys from town. "Where's Jason?"

"I don't know. He hasn't shown up. See that girl over there? That's his sister. Go ask her."

He walked up to her. "Where's Jason?"

"At home."

"Phone him and tell him he's got to come to the church. Brenda Sloan came all the way from Shelby just to see him."

"He can't come. He's got the flu."

"But we came all the way down here to see him."

"Look, I'm not making this up, you know. He's been throwing up all day. He can't even keep ginger ale down."

Kade saw Linda Cooper dancing with another guy. She looked over at Kade and smiled. He nodded back.

Brenda came in the gym. Kade went over to talk to her. "I asked around," he said. "Jason's got the flu."

She tried not to show her disappointment. "It's no big deal."

"Don't give me that. We came all the way down here for you to be with him. The least he could have done was called and told you he was sick."

"It's not his fault. He didn't know I was coming." She looked around. "Well, it's not a complete loss. I see Linda's here. Go dance with her."

"She's already dancing with someone."

"Wait until she isn't and then go ask her."

"What will you do?"

"Don't worry about me. I'll be okay."

Kade went over and asked Linda to dance.

"You came down from Shelby in a snowstorm?" she asked while they danced.

Kade tried to sound macho. "I'm not afraid of a little snow."

"Did Brenda drive?"

"Yeah."

"Why do you keep looking back at her?"

"I want somebody to ask her to dance, that's all. We came all this way so she could dance with Jason Pasco, but he had to ruin everything by getting the flu."

"You like Brenda?"

He didn't know what to say.

"Kade, you're blushing."

"No I'm not."

"Yes you are. Go look in a mirror if you don't believe me. Your face is a bright red."

"That doesn't mean I'm blushing."

"What else could it mean?"

"I just came in from the cold, that's all."

"It happened when I asked if you liked Brenda."

"You don't know anything, Linda, not anything at all."

"I don't see why you're so sensitive about this."

A couple dancing next to them horned in. "What are you two arguing about?" the guy asked.

"I think Kade here has a crush on Brenda Sloan."

"Brenda?" the girl said. "You're kidding. She's a junior, isn't she?" The girl turned to Kade. "What are you?"

"Kade's in the ninth grade, like me," Linda said.

The guy smirked. "Well hey, if you can't get her to go out with you, maybe you can pay her to be your babysitter."

Kade walked off the dance floor and went over to Brenda. "Let's get out of here."

"What's wrong?"

"I just want to get out of here, that's all."

"What about Linda?"

"Forget her. Let's leave this stupid dance."

She thought about it. "Actually, that might not be a bad idea. It's really starting to come down. We'll be better off if we start back before it gets much worse. I brought some other clothes. How about if I go change? You can move the pickup closer to the door if you want. I'll be out in a minute."

"I don't know how to drive, remember?" Kade grumbled. "I'm just the little kid you haul around."

"What's got into you anyway?"

"Go change, will you? I just want to get out of this place."

While he waited for Brenda to finish changing, Linda came over to see him. "Kade, I'm sorry for what happened."

"You and your friends had no right to make fun of me."

"I know that. I'm really sorry. I'll treat you better next time you come to town, okay?"

"Okay."

A minute later Brenda showed up wearing jeans and a Shelby Coyotes sweatshirt. After brushing snow off the windshield, they were on their way again.

Soon they found themselves in the middle of a major winter storm. Snow completely blanketed the road. An hour out of Great Falls, Brenda pulled over and stopped. "We're going to have to get out and put on chains," she said.

"I don't know how."

"I'll show you."

He felt useless. "How come you know everything?"

"Because I'm older." She reached under the seat and pulled out a flashlight. "I need you to come hold the flashlight so I can see what I'm doing. You'd better bundle up. That wind's pretty bad. If it gets too cold, we'll come in and warm up."

Outside, as the storm raged around them, they got into the back of the pickup. He shined the flashlight into the tool compartment while she rummaged around looking for the chains. Her hair was blowing wildly in the wind. The image became imbedded in his mind, and he felt himself slipping into his private world. He knew he would draw a picture of this someday. She found the chains and began pulling them out of the tool compartment. To his vivid imagination they were not chains but the cold brains of a dead metallic monster. She dropped the chains on the ground beside each rear tire.

"Let's go warm up," she yelled above the wind.

They climbed back into the pickup. While they warmed up, he turned on the flashlight so he could see her face more clearly. Her cheeks were flushed, her hair still windblown. The way she looked fascinated him.

"Kade, don't waste the batteries, okay?" she said.

He turned off the flashlight and tried to come back to the real world.

A short time later they went outside. She laid out each chain in the snow just behind the rear tires.

"I need you to start the pickup and back up until I tell you to stop!" she yelled above the roar of the wind.

"I don't know how to drive!" he yelled back.

"This is ridiculous. The next chance I get, I'm teaching you how to drive. All right, I'll go do it. Yell when it rolls this far, okay?"

Okay."

While he waited, he huddled close to the pickup. She started up the motor, and the pickup started rolling back slowly. "Okay!" he shouted.

She got out and knelt down to finish hooking up the chains on the tire. From out of nowhere a large semitruck roared past, scattering in its wake a fury of swirling snow. In an instant it was gone, swallowed up by the thick snow.

"Let's warm up before we do the other tire," she called out.

They climbed in again.

"I'm no good at anything," he said.

She looked over at him. "Hey, it's okay. I had an advantage growing up on a farm. Stick with me, and I'll teach you all I know."

"Thanks for putting up with me."

"No problem. You're a good little guy, Kade."

He wished she hadn't called him little.

A short time later they managed to get the chains on the other tire and then they started off again. They had to go slow because the visibility was so poor. At times they had a difficult time even knowing where the road was.

"This wind is blowing us all over the place," she said. "We need some weight in the back end." She thought about it. "We haven't passed Dutton yet, have we?"

"How should I know? I can't see anything. Why do you want to know?"

"On the way down I noticed the state highway department had a gravel pile next to the road just north of Dutton. We could borrow some and put it in the back end. That'd give us a lot better traction. Of course, we could use snow, but gravel is heavier, and that pile should be close enough to us when we pass by. Keep your eyes peeled for Dutton, okay?"

Half an hour later he saw the sign.

"Okay, it's not much further," she said.

Because he wasn't sure exactly what he was looking for, she spotted it before he did. She slowed down and parked, leaving her lights on in case a car happened to come upon them.

"C'mon, I've got two shovels in the back."

"Isn't this stealing?" Kade asked.

"Look, if we don't get some weight in the rear end, we may not be alive by the time the storm's over. I think the highway department'll understand. C'mon, Mr. Purity of Conscience, let's go to work. You've got to do your share of the work on this job. Don't go telling me you don't know how to use a shovel either."

Because of the bitter winds they had to stop three times to warm up. Finally she said they'd hauled enough, so they threw the shovels in the back and took off again. "This is a lot better," she said.

The storm continued to rage. The drifts in some

places got up to a foot deep. They'd hit the big drifts and slow down, then finally break free again.

"What if we get stuck?" Kade asked.

"Then we dig ourselves out."

"What if it's too deep to dig out?"

"Then we wait until morning, when a snowplow'll come. Whatever happens, there's always a way."

"I wish I were more like you," he said.

She shrugged. "Don't be so hard on yourself. Give yourself some time. I'll teach you all I know, so don't worry about it, okay? You're going to be quite the guy when you grow up."

That made Kade feel better.

Paul and Denise Ellis looked outside at the raging storm. It was snowing so hard they could hardly see the yard light near the barn. And the wind! Paul had never seen a wind like this one tonight, so wild and full of vengeance. He turned to her. "I'll phone the stake center and tell Brenda and Kade to stay in Great Falls at a member's home until the morning."

"That sounds like a good idea."

Nobody answered at the church. Paul called the stake Young Women's president and found out that because of the weather, the leaders had closed the dance and sent everyone home. Those from out of town had gone to members' homes for the night. The Young Women's president called around town for half an hour before she finally found out from Linda Cooper that Brenda and Kade had left for home not long after the dance started. She called Paul and told him.

Paul took the message, then hung up and told Denise.

"So they're out on the road?" she said.

"I guess so."

"We never should have let them go," Denise said.

"I'll call Brenda's parents and see what they say."

Emmet Sloan didn't seem worried. "Brenda knows how to survive in bad weather," he said. "She'll do the right thing. Tell you what, though—I've got a friend who works for the highway department. I'll give him a call and see what he can find out, and then I'll get back to you."

Paul hung up. "He's going to call the highway department and see what he can find out."

"What do you think about Emmet?" she asked.

"He seems okay."

"Since you've been branch president, you've visited most of the families in the branch, but you haven't visited him, have you?"

"No, not yet."

"Why haven't you visited him?"

No answer.

"Is it because he's one of the farmers in trouble with the bank?"

"I can't talk about that."

"I know you can't. I like Susan a lot. She's tried to help me get used to living here. And I think Brenda is good for Kade, even though they are so far apart in age. Emmet is a hard worker, too. They just don't seem like people who should be in financial trouble."

"I really don't want to talk about this."

They waited twenty minutes. Paul was about to phone again when they heard a vehicle pull up into their driveway and stop. Paul went to the door and opened it. Emmet Sloan was stomping his feet on the steps to shake off the snow from his boots and pants. "Think it'll snow?"

They went into the kitchen. "Let me tell you what I found out," Emmet said. "They say the worst of it is just outside of Great Falls. They just closed the road north of Great Falls, but the road crews out of Shelby and Conrad are still working, so there's a good chance

Brenda and Kade will make it through all right. Best thing for us to do is to just stay put and wait."

The pickup was the only vehicle on the road, and their world extended only as far as the headlights reached in the thick, swirling snowstorm. Kade felt abandoned and alone, but also he felt tired. He tried to stay awake but finally fell asleep.

When he woke up, he looked over at Brenda. "I'm sorry I fell asleep," he said.

"Don't worry about it. Hey, guess what, it's getting better. I think there must be a snowplow ahead of us."

A few minutes later they came up behind a snowplow.

"All right!" Brenda exclaimed. "All we've got to do is follow this guy into Shelby. It might be slow, but at least it'll be safe."

They both relaxed. "I'll bet this is more than you bargained for," she said.

"That's for sure."

"Well, we did it. Looks like you're becoming my number one sidekick these days, right?"

"I guess so."

"Do you know what time it is?" she asked.

"No."

"It's after midnight. I'll bet our folks are getting worried."

"I suppose."

"Well, it's almost over. We'll be home before long."

The pressure was off, so they could talk about other things. "You never told me what happened between you and Linda at the dance," she said. "You were talking with her, and then all of a sudden you just walked off and left her standing there. How come?"

"No reason."

"C'mon, Kade, level with me."

He paused. "She and some of her friends were saying I had a crush on you."

"I hope you set 'em right."

"I did."

"Good."

He paused. "I've been thinking about it, though. In a way I guess it might be true."

"It might?"

"A little. But don't worry. I know I'm too young for you."

"That's right, you are."

"There's something I need to tell you, though."

"What?"

"I really like to look at you." He hesitated. "You're very beautiful. In fact, to me you're the most beautiful girl in the world."

She seemed worried. "Kade," she began.

"Don't worry. It's not like I'm in love with you or anything like that. I know I'm too young for you. It's just that I like to look at you. Every day after school I draw a picture of you. I've kept about ten. I just thought you should know."

"Can I see them?"

"I've never shown them to anyone. To tell the truth, I'm kind of embarrassed about all this."

"Why?"

"Sometimes I think there's something wrong with me. I can't seem to stop drawing your face." He cleared his throat. "And I imagine things . . . like one time I drew you as a princess escaping some danger. It was late at night and you were hurrying down a narrow street in England—I guess in the olden times—and you had a veil over your head so nobody would know it was you." He paused. "It sounds like I'm crazy, doesn't it? I don't know what's wrong with me. Sometimes I wish I were more like other people. One thing for sure, I'm not much like the guys on the football team."

"Do you want to be like them?"

"Not really. They're kind of foul-mouthed some-times. So if they're the way a guy is supposed to be, then there's something wrong with me."

"Don't worry about it. You're ten times better than those guys. I'd rather spend time with you than with any of them."

"No kidding?"

"Absolutely."

"And you're not mad at me for drawing your pic-ture?"

"No, of course not."

"Can I ask another question?"

"Sure."

"Are we friends now?" he asked.

"Yeah, I guess we are. That's kind of a surprise in a way, isn't it? I mean, let's face it, you're only a ninth grader. But even so, yeah, I'd say we were friends."

Kade felt terrific.

Paul was amazed at how much confidence Emmet had in Brenda that he could sit there and drink hot chocolate and talk about things other than the storm.

"I should've brought Susan over here with me, but she thought she should stay at home in case Brenda phoned. But since we're neighbors, let's get together sometime."

"Sounds like a good idea," Denise said.

"Great, we'll do it then. Paul, let me ask you a ques-tion. You don't look like a man who would have chosen Shelby as a place to work. In fact, neither of you strikes me as a rural type."

"That's right, we're not," Paul said.

"You never knew Clayton Jones, did you?" Emmet asked. "He was the bank manager before you came."

"No, can't say I did."

"Clayton fit in real good around here. My, but that man loved to loan money. He'd come out every spring and look around the place and make some suggestions of what improvements he thought we should make. We'd say, 'But Clayton, we don't have the money.' And Clayton'd say, 'Hey, no problem. All I've got is time and money.' And so he'd talk us into one thing or another. And then all of a sudden, the bottom dropped out of the farm economy. Clayton retired and moved away, and then you showed up. We were talking about you the other day, Paul. A few of us get together at Pat's Diner some mornings in the winter. Well, we got to talking about the fact that all you do is sit in your office and stare at your computer. We wonder what it is you're doing here in Shelby. We noticed you haven't bought a home yet. Kind of curious, isn't it?"

Paul felt his face getting red. "I didn't think anybody noticed me."

"That's one thing about living in a small town—people notice what you do. As far as any of us can tell, you haven't gone out of your way to make friends with any of us. It makes us wonder what you're up to. I guess we're all a little edgy these days, what with the price of land dropping so low. So when our banker won't talk to us, we get worried. Paul, why don't you get away from your desk one of these days and get to know us a little better."

"That's good advice. I'll do it."

"Good."

"Now can I give you some advice?" Paul asked.

"I suppose."

"We could use you in church on Sundays."

"One of these days when I'm not so busy."

The phone rang. Paul answered. "Emmet, it's for you."

Emmet talked for a while, then hung up. "Good news."

"What?"

"The man running the snowplow south of here radioed in to say Brenda's pickup is following him into town. They should be here in another hour."

"Thank heavens," Denise said.

"When they get to town, he's going to let him stay at his place until morning because the county road out this way hasn't been plowed yet."

Just before they got to town, Brenda asked, "When are you going to let me see the drawings you did of me?"

"There's one thing you gotta understand. My parents don't know about the drawings. I don't want 'em to know either."

"I promise I won't tell anyone about the drawings."

"All right. I'll show them to you whenever you want."

"Thanks."

He didn't want to talk about the drawings anymore. "Turn on the radio," he said. "Let's hear some cowboy music."

"It's growing on you, isn't it," she teased.

"Maybe."

"It is, I can tell. We're going to make a mountain man out of you yet, Kade. You just see if we don't."

"I guess I wouldn't mind that."

"We had ourselves a pretty wild time tonight, didn't we?" she said.

"That's for sure," he said.

As they pulled into Shelby, the operator of the snowplow stopped in the middle of the road and flagged them down. "Brenda?" he asked as she rolled down her window.

"Hi, Mr. Gallagher. So you're the one we've been following all this time, huh?"

"That's right. Say, your dad phoned our dispatcher asking about you, so when I saw your pickup come up behind me, I radioed ahead to let your folks know you were okay. You two'll have to stay the night with my family because the county road isn't plowed yet. Follow me. It's not far."

A few minutes later Brenda and Kade gratefully slipped into sleeping bags in the living room of a small house, Brenda on the couch and Kade on the floor nearby.

Mr. Gallagher went to explain to his wife what was happening. Then he bundled up and left to go back to work.

"Well, pardner, looks like we made it," Brenda said in the dark.

"Yeah, looks like it. Thanks to you." He paused. "Brenda, I've never known anyone like you before."

"My dad says there aren't any more like me. He says they broke the mold after they did me."

"He's right about that."

"I was just joking," she said. "I'm nothing special."

"Don't say that. I didn't even know girls like you existed. You can do just about anything you set your mind to, and you live the way you're supposed to, and you're really good looking." He paused. "If you only knew how you look in the morning when the sun first shines on your face . . ."

She felt uncomfortable hearing him talk like that. "Kade, it's late. We really need to go to sleep now, okay?"

"Okay."

A few minutes later they were both asleep.

By morning there was blue sky and sunshine. The sun reflecting off the snow was so bright it was hard to see.

Mrs. Gallagher made pancakes for her three children and two unexpected guests. Afterwards Kade and Brenda phoned home. Kade's father told him they had cancelled church because of the roads. When Brenda talked to Emmet, he said he would call her back as soon as the county road was plowed.

The morning passed slowly. Kade and Brenda offered to wash the dishes, but Mrs. Gallagher said no. Kade found a pad of paper and drew a picture of each of the children and gave it to them as a present. The youngest girl brought her doll to him and asked him to draw it too. He was just finishing the picture when Emmet called to say the county road had been plowed. Kade and Brenda thanked Mrs. Gallagher, said goodbye, and then left for home.

"You did a good job drawing those pictures," Brenda said.

"Thanks."

"It makes me want to see the ones you've done of me. When can I?"

"We have to be someplace where we can be alone," he said.

"You could come over to my place this afternoon. I'll tell my mom I'm helping you with your homework, and we could go into my mom's sewing room and look at them there. How about if I pick you up around three?"

"Okay. I could bring my books along to make it look like you really are helping me in school."

"Good idea."

A little before three that afternoon he went to the living room, where his mother was practicing the violin. His dad was somewhere doing church work. "I'm going over to Brenda's. We're going to study."

"You and Brenda?" his mother asked.

"What's wrong with that?"

"I would think she'd want to find someone her own age to study with, that's all."

That made Kade mad, but he knew if he made a big fuss she might not let him go at all. "It's just for one assignment."

"All right then."

He went to his closet and pulled down the Monopoly box and put it in his book bag and covered it with a sweatshirt. When Brenda honked for him, he hurried down the stairs, yelled goodbye, then ran through the snow to her pickup.

A few minutes later they entered Brenda's house. "Mom, Kade's here," she called out.

They went into the kitchen, where Brenda's mother was just taking a sheet of chocolate chip cookies out of the oven.

"Kade, you're just in time," she said. "As soon as they cool, I'll have some for you and Brenda."

"Thanks a lot."

Brenda glanced at Kade. "Well, I guess we'd better get started."

They went in the sewing room and Brenda closed the door. "Whenever you're ready."

They sat down. He handed her the Monopoly box. She opened it and took each drawing from the box and looked at it. When she finished, she glanced up at him. "Kade, they're really good. I just wish I was like the girl in these drawings."

He noticed that her eyes were brimming with tears. "You're the most beautiful girl in the world, Brenda. Gosh, don't you know that yet?"

She looked again at one of the drawings. "I think you must be some kind of artistic genius."

"No, not me."

"I'm serious. We need to show these to somebody, a professional artist or a teacher or somebody like that."

"No."

"Why not?"

He thought about what members of the football team might say if they knew about the drawings. "I just don't want anyone to know, that's all."

"All right, if that's the way you feel."

"I'd better go home now."

"Before you go, please have some cookies. My mom baked 'em just for you."

"All right."

They went to the kitchen and sat around the old oak kitchen table and had cookies and milk. A pickup pulled into the place, and Brenda looked out the window. "It's my dad," she said.

Her father came inside. He was in a hurry.

"What's up?" Brenda asked.

"Some of us have decided to go hunt coyotes." He unlocked his gun cabinet and took out a rifle and a box of shells. As he turned around, he looked at the two of them and smiled. "Kind of robbing the cradle there, aren't you, Brenda?"

"I'm just helping Kade with his homework."

"You don't say. Well, I got to go. Brenda, you want to come? It'll be a lot of fun."

"I guess not."

"Doug Albers and his dad'll be there."

"I think I'll stay here with Kade."

"Suit yourself. Oh, since you'll be here anyway, you might as well get something useful done. Do me a favor and hook up the battery charger to your mom's car. When I tried to start it this morning, the battery seemed shot. It's got to last us through the winter."

"Kade and I'll get right to it."

Emmet looked at them and grinned. "A banker's son, huh? I take back what I said before. You marry this kid as soon as he makes it through puberty. We could use a banker in the family."

"Dad, don't be such a tease."

He put a box of shells in his coat pocket and tucked the gun under one arm. "Well, I'm on my way. Doug's going to be real disappointed you're not coming." He left.

"Sorry," she said to Kade. "My dad likes to kid around a lot."

"That's okay."

"Do you want to help me hook up the battery charger for the pickup?"

"I don't know how."

"I'll show you what to do."

"Okay."

They used her pickup to push her mother's car into the barn. A minute later they had the hood open. "Okay," she said, "the first thing we have to do is decide which is the hot side and which is ground."

He was puzzled. "Ground is what we're standing on."

She smiled. "It's something else when it comes to electricity."

As they worked, he asked her why she hadn't gone

with her dad when she knew Doug Albers would be there too.

"What's so special about Doug Albers?" she asked.

"He's one of the best players on the football team. He'll probably get a big football scholarship when he goes to college next year. He's got a great build, and he's good looking too. After a game there's always girls waiting around for him outside the locker room. How come you're not impressed with him?"

"Doug and I used to be friends, but we're not anymore."

They went back to the house, and she showed him several family scrapbooks, going back to when her dad was a boy living in the same house. "Our family's been on this land since the area was first opened up for homesteading in 1910," she said. "The first house burned up in 1940, so this place was built. My dad was even born in this house. After high school he joined the Navy. That's where he met my mother. She was a member of the Church living in San Diego with her parents. They weren't too happy about her going with a nonmember. She had him take the lessons, and he got baptized before they got married. After he got out of the service, they moved back here and helped out until my grandparents retired and moved away. Then my dad took over the place."

"So are you going to take over someday?" he asked.

She paused. "I'm not sure. My mom wants me to go to BYU before I decide."

She gave him a ride home a little before six o'clock. His parents had eaten without him. He went to his room and put the Monopoly box containing the drawings back on the shelf of his closet, then went downstairs.

His mother put his supper in the microwave for him. "Did you have a nice time at Brenda's?" she asked.

"Yeah, she showed me how to hook up a battery charger."

"I hope you got your schoolwork done too."

"Oh, yeah, that too." After he finished eating, he said, "I'm going up to my room to study."

"I've never seen you spend so much time alone in your room before."

"It's a hard year for me."

She gave him a strange look. "Yes, I think it must be."

After school on Monday, as soon as they turned onto the county road, Brenda pulled over and stopped. "You ready to learn how to drive? There's not much traffic here usually."

"Really?"

"Sure, no problem."

They traded places. "Okay," she said, "that's the clutch over there and the brake next to it, and that's the gas. You push that when you want to go faster."

"I know all that."

"Good. Shifting gears is the tricky part. What you have to do is shove the clutch down to the floor, put it in the gear you want, and then take the clutch out at the same time you give it more gas. Okay, now you try it."

He tried it but killed the engine.

"No problem. Try it again."

He killed it again.

After five tries, he managed to keep the engine going. They started moving slowly down the road.

"All right, Kade! You did it."

He felt terrific. He was actually driving.

"You want to put it in second now?" she asked a few seconds later.

"No, this is okay."

She paused. "But we're only going ten miles an hour. We could do a lot better in second."

"Is second going to be as hard as first?"

"No, not really."

He thought about it. "I guess I'll try then."

She put her hand over his on the gear-shift rod and helped him shift into second. Now they were going twenty miles an hour. Kade hadn't felt so excited since he was little on Christmas morning.

She helped him shift into third.

He spotted a pickup coming toward them fast. He slowed down and pulled to the right, nearly off the road.

"We're allowed half the road, Kade. Don't pull over so far. And either give it more gas or shift into second. The engine's lugging down."

Kade overdid it and pulled into the center of the road. The driver of the pickup frantically honked for them to get out of his way. They narrowly missed having a collision.

"Well, I think maybe that's enough for today," she said, relieved to still be alive.

Kade slowed down and killed the engine.

"Thanks a lot," he said.

"No problem."

After that she let him drive partway home every day. He didn't dare drive all the way because his parents didn't want him driving until he turned fifteen.

From the beginning Paul Ellis had known what needed to be done. There were certain guidelines the bank had adopted to help in its decisions. One was that when a person's outstanding loans exceeded 50 percent of his equity, he became a bad risk for the bank. It was a simple policy, not open to much interpretation.

Up until last year the country had been in an inflationary spiral. Many experts felt that it made sense to borrow during a time of inflation because you always paid back your loan with cheaper money. Besides that, the land kept increasing in value every year, so your equity continued to grow. Since it made sense to borrow, lending institutions found themselves competing with each other for loans. Clayton Jones, the man Paul replaced as bank manager, had gone out of his way to talk farmers into borrowing money for new equipment and improvements.

And then suddenly, within one year, the value of land dropped dramatically nationwide. Some farmers saw the value of their land drop to half of what it had been. This meant a farmer might find that almost overnight he had become a bad risk to his lenders. Strangely enough, it had nothing to do with his skill as a farmer.

A less thorough man than Paul might have shown up in Shelby and within a week taken steps to reduce the bank's bad loans. But Paul couldn't do that. He felt a responsibility to see what he could to help those who had been doing business with the bank for many years.

He took Emmet's suggestion and started visiting families who had large loans with the bank. He found himself impressed with these people. They were hard-working and honest and valued their families. For the most part their farms had been in the same family for generations.

One day when he got back to his office after spending the morning out talking to people, there was a message on his desk that Dwight Allen from the corporate office had called. He sat down at his desk and punched the phone number.

A minute later Dwight came on the line. "Paul, I was beginning to wonder if you'd been eaten by a bear. I haven't heard from you lately."

"Sorry. I've been visiting some of the farms in the area."

"I haven't seen much paperwork coming from your office. What's the delay?"

"It's more complicated than I thought."

"Look, Paul, you're too late for the regional manager slot in Indiana. It's already filled. Finish up there. Let's see some action from you, okay?"

"These are good, hardworking people," Paul said. "Their whole lives are in farming. It goes back from father to son for generations."

"We run a business, not a historical society. I'm worried about you. Don't let them turn you into another Clayton Jones."

"I'll do what's best for the bank, but not until I have all the facts."

"Don't take too much time, or you'll find yourself stranded in Montana for the rest of your career."

Kade enjoyed being equipment manager for the football team. He liked spending his free periods in the laundry room. It gave him a place to study as well as let him do something useful at the same time. The team accepted him. Most of them would at least nod when they saw him in the hall. The coach appreciated Kade's dependability. One time at a pep rally he introduced him as the best equipment manager the team ever had.

Sometimes Marvin Mudlin would come in the laundry room and they'd talk. One time he brought in a soccer ball used in the girls' gym classes. "Show me what you can do."

Kade put on a show, moving the ball with just his feet.

"That's good, Kade. Too bad it's worthless out here in Montana."

"Yeah, too bad."

The buzzer on the dryer went off. Kade took some things out and then sat down again. He took off his glasses. "Do you think I'll look better with contacts?"

"Sure you will."

"I hope I look older, too."

"How old you want to look?"

"I dunno. Sixteen, I guess."

"Why sixteen?"

He thought about saying how much he was begin-ning to like Brenda, but didn't because he was afraid it would get back to her. "No reason. I wish I could get contacts now. My parents won't help pay for 'em be-cause they say there's nothing wrong with my glasses. I wish they'd change their minds."

"Hey, my parents don't pay for things I want," Mar-vin said. "I have to earn it all or go without. I figure that's part of being a man."

After that, Kade quit bothering his parents about contact lenses. He just kept saving his money.

In November Brenda asked Kade if he wanted to go deer hunting with her and Emmet on Saturday.

"I've never gone hunting before."

"It doesn't matter."

"All right, I'll go then."

The night before they left, Kade set his alarm for five o'clock. When the alarm went off, he got up immediately and took a shower. When he came out of the bathroom, his father was in the kitchen reading. "You took a shower before going hunting?" his father asked with a smile.

"Yeah, so?"

His father smiled. "Nothing."

After he got dressed, Kade sat down at the kitchen table and had breakfast.

"I've never taken you hunting before," Paul said.

"That's because you don't hunt."

"Do you wish I did?"

"Not really."

"We don't do much together like we used to, do we."

"We set up chairs for church on Sundays."

"That's true. It's just that time is going so fast. I always thought that we'd be closer at this time in your life than we are."

"Most of the things that interest you I don't care about. Like investments and loans."

"I didn't always used to be interested in those things."

Kade heard the sound of someone pulling into the driveway. He shoved a spoonful of cereal into his mouth, then stood up. "I'd better go brush my teeth."

"Of course. You don't want to offend the deer with bad breath, do you," his dad said with a smile.

It was still cold and dark as Kade trudged through the snow to the pickup.

"How's the mighty hunter today?" Emmet said.

Because Kade was shorter than Brenda, he had to sit in the middle, dodging the gearshift lever. "Mr. Sloan, I really want to thank you for taking me along."

"Hey, no problem. And just call me Emmet. That's my name."

"I think I'll call you Emmet too," Brenda said.

"Hey, you call me honorable father."

She smiled. "Oh sure, like I'm really going to do that."

They drove for a long time. Kade fell asleep. When he woke up, he realized his head had been resting on Brenda's shoulder.

"Well, Mountain Man, you all done with your nappy pooh?" Emmet said. He sang the first line of "Put Your Head on My Shoulder."

Kade blushed and looked over at Brenda. She didn't seem bothered about it one way or the other.

It was a gray, cloudy day. The pickup climbed through the mountains on a gravel road, with Emmet balancing a mug of coffee in his hand while he drove. "We're almost there," he said.

It started raining, and the wipers flapped back and forth across the windshield. As they continued to climb, the rain turned to snow.

Brenda pulled out a package of donuts and passed them around.

"You've never been hunting before, is that right, Kade?" Emmet asked.

"Yes."

"Well, we have kind of a tradition in our family. The first buck we get, when we're cleaning it out, we cut off a slice of deer heart, and each hunter takes a piece and eats it raw. That wouldn't bother you any, would it? I mean, you're not afraid of eating a piece of raw deer heart, are you?"

There was a long silence and then Kade gulped. "I guess not."

"What if it's still beating?" Emmet asked.

"Dad, you quit your teasing. I mean it, too."

Emmet was laughing. "He fell for it."

"I knew you were kidding."

"Sure you did," Emmet said.

A few minutes later he stopped to let Brenda and Kade out. "Brenda, you know what to do, don't you?"

"Sure, no problem."

She turned and removed her rifle from the gun rack.

"Be careful," Emmet called out. "Make some noise so bears can hear you coming. This is grizzly country."

Kade gulped.

"Kade, you're not afraid of a grizzly bear, are you?" Emmet said.

Kade smiled faintly.

Emmet drove off, leaving them standing there in the snow.

"Don't let my dad get to you."

"Was he kidding about this being grizzly country?"

"No, but don't worry, we won't see any. What we're going to do now is hike up that ridge. My dad'll be waiting on top. The idea is that we chase the deer toward him. C'mon, let's go."

There was about two inches of new snow on the trail. Kade imagined a bear behind every bush and tree along the way.

"I think my dad likes you, Kade."

"He has a strange way of showing it."

"Oh, that's just him. You'll get used to it." She paused. "I had a little brother who died when he was just a couple of weeks old. I think you and he would be about the same age. After that my mom couldn't have any more kids. Dad's sort of raised me like a son, but still, I think he wishes he had one for real. I think that's why he's kind of taken to you."

"I don't see how he could want anybody else, seeing how he's got you."

"That's nice of you to say. Thanks."

He paused. "There's a lot of other things I could say about you."

"Like what?"

He paused, not knowing whether to say it or not. Finally he decided to say it. "I've thought a lot about it lately, and I think I love you."

She stopped walking. "Look, Kade, don't try to make our friendship into something it can't ever be, or this'll turn sour on us and I'll have to quit seeing you. Okay?"

"But I think about you all the time. The way you look in the morning when the sun is on your face. Sometimes when you sing along to a song on the radio, I pretend you're singing it to me."

"Stop it, Kade. I really mean it. You can't go talking like that. It's not right."

"Why isn't it right?"

"Because you're just a kid." She glanced at him. He looked devastated. "You're not going to cry, are you?" she asked.

"You had to say that, didn't you?"

"I'm sorry. I shouldn't have said that."

They walked for a long time without saying anything. And then she said, "I think we should sing a song. It'll let the bears know we're coming. What do you want to sing?"

"I don't feel like singing."

"Well, how about 'We Thank Thee, O God, for a Prophet.' " She started out.

He tried to sing an octave lower to show her how low his voice was, but then decided it wouldn't make any difference to her anyway, so he sang in unison with her.

Four deer, startled by their noise, ran out of the woods into a clearing. Kade stopped to watch them. They were so graceful. There was a fence in front of them. They jumped over it in one graceful leap.

He took in the scene—the deer, the snowy field, Brenda with a red hunting vest over her coat, her face flushed from their exercise, snow gathering on her hat, her eyes somber, her expression subdued and a little sad.

A short time later they heard three shots. Each shot came in multiple echoes to their ears.

"That was my dad. C'mon, let's go see how he did."

They hurried to where the sound had come from. When they made it to the top of the ridge, they saw three deer on the ground. Emmet was bending over one of them, slicing its throat. The blood from each of the other deer stained the snow.

"Good shooting, Dad!" Brenda called out.

"Sure, what'd you expect?" Emmet said. He stood up. "Well, Kade, one of these is yours. Which one do you want?"

"It doesn't matter."

"Why don't you take that one over there?"

"Okay."

"You know how to clean a deer?"

"No."

"Brenda, why don't you show him?"

"Sure. Come here, Kade, and watch me do mine."

Kade knelt beside her as she dressed out the deer. "Do you want to save the heart?" Brenda called out to her father.

"No, leave it for the bears, or else give it to Kade."

She laughed. "If you don't quit your teasing, Kade'll never come anywhere with us again."

Brenda finished her deer, then helped him do his. Afterwards she said, "Dad, Kade did a good job, for his first time."

"Well, that's just great."

Kade got home by noon. His parents were at stake leadership meeting in Great Falls. Emmet helped him hang the deer in the garage, and then they left.

Kade fixed himself some soup and a couple of sandwiches. After he finished eating, he took a shower and then went to his room and sat down and drew a picture of Brenda the way she had looked when they were hiking. But it was no good, and he ended up throwing it away.

He wandered out to the garage and stood in front of the deer as it hung from the rafters. He remembered how it had been when it was running and jumped the fence. Even though he had enjoyed his first hunting trip, he felt bad to have had a part in killing something so beautiful.

The next week Brenda went out of her way to be nice to Kade because she wanted him to understand that she did enjoy having him as a friend, even though that's all it could ever be between them.

On Saturday her mother asked her to go to town to buy groceries. She asked Kade if he wanted to go along for the ride. He said yes.

Though it was still cold and the ground was covered with snow, the wind wasn't blowing, so if you stood in the sun long enough it would warm your face.

In the grocery story Kade helped her find the things she needed. By the time they were finished, they'd filled two shopping carts. After they were done, she suggested they drop by Pat's Diner and have some hot chocolate. He offered to pay for hers, but she said she had enough money.

The place was crowded with farm families who'd come to town. The booths were all full, but they managed to find a couple of seats at the counter. The place smelled of hotcakes and bacon and sausage.

While they sipped their hot chocolate, Doug Albers came over. "Hey, Brenda, you want to go bowling?"

"Now?"

"Sure, why not?"

"We just got groceries."

"So?"

"The milk'll freeze if I leave it in the pickup very long."

"We can put it inside."

"Then the ice cream'll melt. Besides I need to get Kade home."

"How about tonight then?"

She hesitated. "I don't know."

"Come on, Brenda. You never do anything anymore."

"Will you be getting drunk tonight like you usually do?" she asked.

"I don't drink that much."

"Just every weekend, that's all."

"Look, I promise not to touch a drop. What do you say?"

"I'm not going to park with you either, so you can just get that out of your mind too."

"Now why would you even bring that up?"

"I heard about you and Traci Hunter after the homecoming game."

"What'd you hear?"

"That she had to slap your face to get you to back off."

"Look, I had too much to drink. I didn't know what I was doing. It'll never happen again."

"You've got to respect the way I believe, Doug."

"I do, honest. C'mon, Brenda, you need a man in your life, not some twerp who tags around after you like a puppy dog."

"Don't pick on Kade. He's okay. He's more of a man than you are."

Doug smirked. "Get serious. C'mon, how about it? I'll pick you up at seven. We'll go bowling and then go and get a pizza and a pitcher of root beer. No drinking and no parking. Whataya say?"

Brenda sighed. "All right, but you'd better watch yourself, Doug, or this'll be the last time I ever go out with you."

"No problem. See you tonight." He went back to the table he'd come from.

They went outside and started back home. Kade was so furious, he could hardly speak.

"It's just bowling," she said after several minutes of silence.

"Why are you going out with him? He's not even a member of the Church."

That made her mad. "Who around here is? Nobody. I think it's okay for church leaders to tell kids in Utah to only date members, but out here, who else have I got to choose from?"

"There's Jason Pasco."

"Jason Pasco," she grumbled. "Forget Jason Pasco. I could wait ten years, and you think he'd ever phone or write me a letter or let me know he cares about me? No way. He's useless to me. What am I supposed to do—go into hibernation until I graduate from high school? Well, I can't. I like guys, Kade. I'm attracted to them. I like being around a guy my age. Is there something wrong with that?"

"What about me?"

She sighed. "Look, we've gone through this before. I like you and all, and you're really a nice guy, but it's just not the same."

He turned away and pouted.

A few minutes later she said, "Gosh, Kade, I wish you wouldn't be so sensitive all the time. Look, I'm sorry if I hurt your feelings, but I have to let you know how it is for me."

As soon as she pulled in front of his house, he jumped out and hurried inside.

The next day was Sunday. Kade was curious to know how her date with Doug had been but he was still so mad that he snubbed her at church.

On Monday she picked him up for seminary. They didn't talk much. She tried to get some kind of conversation going, but he wouldn't cooperate. During the seminary lesson Sister Simmons said that members of the Church should only date members. Kade turned around to glare at Brenda.

After seminary Kade had to ride to school with Brenda and Melissa, but he refused to sit in the middle again. "It's my turn to ride shotgun today," he declared. He got his way.

When they pulled into the school parking lot, he noticed Doug getting out of his Ford Bronco. He started over to see Brenda.

Kade and Melissa left before Doug got there. Once they were inside the building, Kade looked back. Doug had his arm draped around Brenda.

"What's the matter, Kade? Are you jealous?" Melissa said.

"Why do you have to be such a witch all the time?" Kade grumbled. He turned to leave.

When Kade went out to the parking lot after school, he found Doug and Brenda together in her pickup. Doug was in the driver's seat. Kade was sure they'd been kissing. He got in and shut the door.

"So, Kade, what's this?" Doug said. "You come to watch?"

Kade was furious. He swore at Doug. It was the first time he'd ever sworn in his life.

Doug laughed. "The twerp's got a big mouth, don't he? Kade, maybe I should pound some sense into that pea-brain of yours."

"Anytime you want to try, just let me know."

Doug laughed. "Hey, like I'm really worried."

"Doug, you'd better go," Brenda said. "I need to get home and help my dad."

"All right. I'll call you tonight. See ya." He gave her a quick kiss and left.

Five minutes later they were on the road heading home.

"It sure didn't take him long, did it," Kade said bitterly.

"Back off, Kade. It's none of your business."

"He goes around acting like he owns you. I bet you let him kiss you anytime he wants, don't you."

"Look, after you grow up a little, we'll talk about this, but until then, just back off, okay?"

"What does he think about the Church?"

"It hasn't come up."

"I bet it hasn't."

"What do you mean by that?"

"You're willing to give up everything you've been taught just to please him, aren't you. Well, just make sure you don't get pregnant."

She slammed on the brakes. They came to a sudden stop. "Get out!"

"What?"

"I said get out, and I mean it! Nobody talks to me that way."

"I can't get out here. It's snowing, and it's a long ways home."

"I don't care. I want you out!"

He opened the door and stepped down. "What am I supposed to do out here in the middle of nowhere?"

"It's your choice—either freeze to death or walk home."

He slammed the door as hard as he could, and she drove off. He was alone. The wind was blowing snow in his face, and it was cold. He was suddenly worried.

A quarter mile down the road she stopped and put the pickup in reverse, then backed up to where he was and stopped. She leaned over and opened his door. "Get in," she ordered.

He got in. She took off again, and they rode in silence. "I'm sorry for talking to you the way I did," he said.

"You should be. I can't believe you said that to me. You don't know anything, Kade. Not anything at all."

As soon as they pulled up to his house, he got out and left without even saying goodbye.

For the rest of the week they didn't talk much. Every morning Doug was waiting for her when she pulled into the parking lot.

On Friday night there was a home game played in a snowstorm. Shelby easily won it 42 to 10. In the locker room after the game, as members of the team shouted and punched each other in victory, Kade quietly went about the business of gathering muddy uniforms from team members.

On Saturday night he watched TV until eleven and then went to bed. A little before one o'clock he heard a soft thump on the side of the house.

"Kade," someone called out.

He got out of bed and looked out. Brenda was standing below him in the snow, throwing snowballs at the house. He opened the window. Cold air poured onto his bare toes. "What do you want?" he asked.

"I need to talk to you."

"Okay, just a minute." He got dressed, then tiptoed down the stairs. He grabbed his coat, slipped on his boots, and went outside.

She was standing there waiting for him. "I left my pickup down on the main road so we wouldn't wake your folks. I thought maybe we could drive around for a while."

They walked down the snow-packed driveway to her pickup. She'd left the motor running, so it was warm inside. They took off down the road. "I went out with Doug tonight."

"How was it?"

"Awful. He took me to a party at his friend's house. The parents were gone for the weekend. Someone brought a keg of beer, and everyone was drinking except me. I felt so out of it. I tried to get Doug to stop drinking but he wouldn't. We danced for a while, and then he asked me to go upstairs with him to one of the bedrooms. I told him no. He got mad at me. I told him to stop acting like a fool, but he just kept at it. Finally I made him take me home. When I got home, my dad asked me if I'd had a nice time, and I told him that we'd had an argument. I could tell my dad was disappointed. I think he'd like Doug and me to get married so we can take over the farm someday."

"Did you tell your dad what happened?"

"No, I can't talk to him about things like that." She paused. "I went to bed and tried to sleep, but it was no use, so I got dressed and came over here. I'm sorry for dumping this all on you, but I feel so awful and mixed up and I don't know who else to talk to. I just don't know what to do."

"Do you still like Doug?"

"I don't know. Most of the time he's really nice. He called me every night last week, and he was there every morning when I got to school. He walked me to my classes, and we ate lunch together. A couple of nights ago he came over, and we all just sat around and talked. Doug and my dad really get along." She sighed. "But Doug has no interest in the Church and I don't think I could ever get him to stop drinking." She hesitated. "There's another thing. Doug says there's nothing wrong if a couple in high school go ahead and . . . rush things." She paused. "Do you know what I mean by that?"

"Yes."

"Kade, what do you think I should do?"

"What do you want to happen?"

"I want Doug to quit drinking and join the Church."

"Do you think that'll ever happen?"

It took a long time before she answered. "No, not really." She sighed. "Most of the time he's good to me, and I like being with him. But when he starts drinking, things get ugly. The thing is, I'm not sure I can go with Doug and still maintain my standards." She paused. "I guess that means I'd better break up with him."

"I suppose."

"But it's not fair, Kade. If I decide to only date Mormons, then I won't ever go out because there's nobody around here for me."

"We could start going to the youth dances in Great Falls again."

"How can you say that after we nearly got killed the last time we went to a dance in Great Falls?"

He smiled. "I know, but even so, it was kind of fun."

"So I guess it's just you and me again," she said.

"I guess so. Look, I'm really sorry I'm not . . . " He

paused for a long time. It was painful for him to say it. " . . . that I can't be what you need."

"Oh gosh, Kade, you're everything a girl could want except for the fact that you're too young for me."

"There's probably not much I can do about that, is there."

"No, but at least we can be friends. You know, if it weren't for you, I'd be all alone."

"Me too," he said. "You're the best friend I've ever had."

"The same for me. Well, I'd better get you back before your parents wake up and wonder where you've gone. Thanks for talking to me."

"Sure, anytime."

Later in his room he couldn't sleep, so he got out of bed and went to his desk and drew a picture of Brenda the way it had been as she drove, her face barely visible by the dashboard lights, the opposites of light and shadow repeatedly playing against each other as she moved her head closer to and then farther away from the light.

After football practice on Monday, Doug, bitter at having been dropped by Brenda, started bragging about his exploits with her, telling lies about what they'd done on their dates.

Kade had stayed after school to get caught up after Friday night's game. Because it had been such a mess out on the field Friday night, he had to wash some things twice. He overheard what Doug was saying and came out into the locker room. "None of what you're saying about Brenda is true."

"How do you know? You weren't there. You don't know what happened."

"Brenda's not that kind of girl."

"She is now."

"You're lying. Take back what you said."

"No. What I said is all true."

"Take it back, I said."

Doug smiled. "You think you're man enough to make me?" He cuffed Kade on the side of his face, but not hard enough to hurt him—he was just having fun. "Let's see how fast you are. Stop this." He tapped Kade on the mouth. "Here's another one. You ready for it?"

He hit him again, a little harder, this time on the nose. Kade's nose began to bleed.

Kade swung as hard as he could. Doug blocked the punch. "You got to be faster than that. C'mon, try it again. This time I'll close my eyes. Maybe you'll get lucky. See what you can do." Doug dropped his guard and stuck out his chin and closed his eyes. "C'mon, see if you can hit me with my eyes closed."

Kade threw a punch. Doug grabbed his wrist. "Whoops! Not fast enough, even with my eyes closed. What a loser! You're not much good for anything, are you!" He paused. "Oh, there's one thing you're good for, isn't there? Sure there is. You're good at washing clothes. Here, Kade, I've got a little present for you." Doug turned to pick up parts of his practice uniform. Kade, seeing an opportunity, lunged and caught him off balance. Doug's shoulder hit the lockers. The smile on his face was gone. "You want to play rough? Okay by me. Looks like I gotta teach you a lesson, don't I!" He shoved Kade backwards. Kade managed to stay on his feet, but Doug kept coming.

Suddenly Marvin Mudlin came behind Doug and put a hammerlock on him. As hard as Doug tried, he couldn't break loose. The more he struggled, the more pressure Marvin put on his neck.

"You leave Kade alone, you hear me?" Marvin said.

Doug, desperate for breath, nodded.

Marvin let up some on the hammerlock. "Now take back what you said about Brenda."

Doug spoke softly. "It was all a lie. Nothing happened between us."

"Louder," Marvin said.

"Nothing happened between us. I was lying about everything."

"All right then. Now you listen to me. You ever mess with Kade again and I'll come looking for you. You got that?"

Doug nodded again. Marvin shoved him away, and he hurried to his locker, picked up his things, and walked out.

Marvin walked up to Kade. "You either got to get a whole lot stronger or else learn to back down once in a while. The way you're going, you're not going to make it out of ninth grade."

The football season for Shelby High School ended with the quarter-final state championship playoff game the second weekend in November, held in the field-house at Montana State University in Bozeman. Kade traveled with the team. They went by chartered bus and stayed in a motel. Kade and Marvin roomed together.

It was an exciting game. The score was tied going into the final two minutes. The opposing team ate up the clock with running plays, advancing the ball to the twenty-yard line. With twenty seconds left, they kicked a field goal and won the game.

It was a tough way to end a good season.

On the trip home, Kade and Marvin sat together. "If you ask me, you need to start lifting weights," Marvin said. "You need to put some meat on those bones of yours. Like if your mom ever fixes mashed potatoes, eat as much as you can stand. That's what I did, and look at me."

"What if I don't want to be as big as you?"

"If you were, I think it might change Brenda's mind about you."

Kade blushed. "We're just friends."

"Don't give me that. I've seen the way you look at her in school."

"It's no use, Marvin. She's older than me."

"So what? Let's say you got yourself a set of weights and worked out every day and got, you know, in really good shape. I don't think her being older would matter

then. It can't hurt to try, can it? Ask your folks for a set
of barbells for Christmas."

Kade did ask about getting barbells for Christmas.
His mother said they were too dangerous because he
might get a hernia.

Dwight Allen hadn't called for a while, which made
Paul feel that if he wasn't careful, he might find himself
permanently trapped in a dead-end job in Shelby.

He realized that Denise wasn't very happy living in
Montana. She missed playing in a symphony orchestra,
as she'd done in other towns they'd lived in. But that
wasn't all. In Illinois they'd had season tickets to the
Chicago Symphony, they'd been in a ward with a brand
new building, and when they went shopping, they'd
had more of a choice of what to buy.

As time went on, Paul found himself feeling more
of a victim himself. Because of falling land prices, farmers who would ordinarily be able to weather bad eco-
nomic times were now in serious trouble. Everything
depended on the loan-to-equity ratio.

He had prepared a list of farmers in trouble. One on
the list was Emmet Sloan, and another was Marvin Mudlin's father.

Paul worried how Kade would take it if the families
of his two closest friends were refused operating loans
for the next growing season.

During the two-week Christmas break, Kade went
over to Brenda's house every day. Sometimes the two
of them went with Emmet into town. Kade liked being
around Emmet because he knew how to do things that
men traditionally do — auto and diesel mechanics, wiring
a home, plumbing, hunting, fishing, football, basket-
ball, baseball.

Brenda's grandparents drove up from Arizona for Christmas. They had farmed in Shelby for forty years until finally they retired and Emmet took over.

When they met Kade, Brenda's grandfather asked him where he lived. He told them. "Oh, that's the Aldrich farm. Whatever happened to them?"

"They went broke and had to sell out," Brenda said.

"Poor management," her grandfather said.

"Not necessarily," Emmet said.

"How else can you explain it? A farm five miles away goes belly up. They have the same soil as us, they grow the same crops, they get the same weather we do. What else can it be except poor management?" With that, the subject was closed.

One day when Brenda was fixing a pie and didn't want to leave until it was done, Kade rode into town with Emmet, just the two of them.

"What's it like being the son of a banker?" Emmet asked as they bounced down the country road.

"It's all right, I guess." Kade paused. "Except my dad's not as much fun to be with as you."

"Why's that?"

"He doesn't know how to do anything useful."

Emmet laughed. "He might not agree with you about that."

"I know, but it's true. Like yesterday when you showed Brenda and me how to weld. My dad never does stuff like that. He pays to have people do things around the house. I've learned more practical things from you and Brenda than I ever have at home."

"But, Kade, you got to realize your dad's a busy man."

"Yeah, sure he is. He's the branch president and he's trying to raise some money to build a church, but first they got to get more people to go to church, so he spends a lot of time going around asking inactives to go to church."

"Like me?"

"Yeah. How come you never go to church?"

"Force of habit, I guess. Maybe I'll start coming out the first of the year."

"My dad'd like that a lot. And it wouldn't hurt if you quit drinking coffee either."

"There's no pleasing you, is there?" Emmet said.

"No, I guess not."

"Kade, you're quite the guy, you know that?"

"Me?"

"Yes, you."

"Not me."

"What do you mean, not you?"

"I wear these stupid glasses."

"It doesn't matter. What matters is what's inside you."

"I've lost every fight I've ever been in."

"Why's that?"

"Because I'm not as big as the guys I fight."

Emmet grinned. "That's easy to fix—pick on smaller guys." He glanced over at Kade. "Look, don't worry about it. One day you'll hit a growth spurt and just shoot up. That's what happened to me."

"I was thinking that if I had a set of barbells and worked out every day . . . " He sighed. "I asked my mom about it, but she said no. She said I'd hurt myself, but I know that'd never happen."

"Maybe Santa Claus'll bring you a set of barbells."

He scoffed. "Yeah, sure."

They stopped at a farm co-op for supplies and then dropped by Pat's Diner. They sat down at a booth with some friends of Emmet.

"What's this, Emmet? You adopt a kid or something?" one asked.

"No, this is our neighbor's boy, Kade Ellis."

"The banker's kid?"

"Yeah."

"You're the one who knocked my son on his can in the locker room, aren't you," one of the men commented.

"Are you Mr. Mudlin?" Kade asked.

"That's right."

"Kade, I haven't heard this story before," Emmet said.

"There's not much to tell," Kade said. "When school started in the fall, Marvin kept snapping me with a towel after gym class. One day I decided I wasn't going to take it any longer. We got into a fight until the gym teacher broke it up."

"You did the right thing," Mr. Mudlin said. "You can't let people push you around."

"I know. Actually it turned out okay. Marvin and I are real good friends now."

"He talks about you sometimes. I think you've been good for him."

The conversation drifted to other topics. Kade quietly drank his hot chocolate and ate his doughnut. He felt like he'd been accepted into a select group of the men who did the most important work in the world. These were men who could make things happen.

Kade's father walked in the cafe with another man, both of them in overcoats and three-piece blue suits. Kade had never seen the other man. He looked like someone who was used to getting his way.

The two men sat at a table near the back of the cafe. Nobody called out to them as they'd done when Emmet walked in. But even so, everyone had their eyes on them, as if they were the enemy. It was something Kade picked up on. Being there with these men made it seem as if he were looking at his father for the first time. Compared to the men he was with, his dad seemed stiff and formal and official.

Emmet put his arm around Kade's shoulder and

leaned over. He spoke confidentially. "Kade, are you going to go over and say hello to your dad?"

It seemed too much to ask, to let everyone know that the man in the three-piece suit was his father.

"No, that's okay. We see each other at home all the time."

"Kade, you've got to go over and say hello."

"What for?"

"Because if he sees you walking out of here, he might think you're ashamed of him."

Kade sighed. "Nobody here likes my dad, do they?"

"It's nothing personal. We're just worried about losing something we've worked for all our lives." Emmet squeezed his shoulder. "Go say hello. C'mon, you've got to do it."

Emmet stood up and let Kade out of the booth. The walk up the aisle seemed to take forever. He felt as though everyone was staring at him. His father looked up from the report the other man was showing him.

"Hi, Dad," Kade said softly.

"Kade, what are you doing in town?"

"Emmet brought me."

"Kade, I'd like you to meet Dwight Allen. He flew in today to help me with my work. He's from the corporate office in Chicago."

"Hello, Mr. Allen."

"Sit down and let me buy you something to eat."

"No, thanks. I've got to go. Emmet's about to leave now."

Dwight smiled. "Your dad says you're a fan of the Chicago Bears."

"That's right."

"If I can ever get your family out to Illinois again, I'll take you over and let you meet some of the team."

"I'd like that. Well, I'd better go now. 'Bye."

"Goodbye, Kade," his father said.

Kade walked back. Emmet had already paid and was

waiting at the door for him. They went outside. Kade looked up at the time-and-temperature sign on the bank. It read ten below zero. They got into the pickup. Emmet started it up. "It was the right thing to do," he said.

"I suppose," Kade said in the same drawl Brenda used.

That evening Dwight Allen offered to take the family out for supper. He asked if there were any really good places to eat in town. Kade's mother suggested the Dixie Inn.

Kade didn't like Mr. Allen because all he did was to brag about how wonderful he was. When the waitress came to take their order, he tried to order in French, until the waitress finally admitted she didn't understand.

"How can you have French cuisine here and not speak French?" Mr. Allen asked.

"Hey, I just bring the food to the table."

After the waitress left, Mr. Allen made fun of her. "She wouldn't last a day in a good restaurant in Chicago."

"She's not in Chicago," Kade mumbled, but not loud enough to be picked up by anyone.

Over dessert, Mr. Allen turned to Denise. "We hope to get you and Paul out of Montana soon. We'll get you back to civilization where there's culture and the arts and a symphony orchestra you can play in."

"Well, that'd be nice," Denise said, "although there are some advantages to living here."

Paul was surprised at her response. "Like what?"

"Well, the people here are friendly and honest and hard-working."

"Kade, you can't possibly be happy here," Mr. Allen said.

"Why's that?"

"Well, for one thing, riding through town today I

didn't see a McDonald's or a Burger King. And I know teenagers can't survive without fast food."

Kade didn't appreciate Mr. Allen thinking he knew everything there was to know.

Mr. Allen continued. "I'm sure you'd like it better in a place where there's more things to do for someone your age."

Kade had had it. "What makes you such an authority on my life?"

His parents were shocked. "Kade, is that any way to talk?" his mother said. "I think you'd better apologize."

"I'm sorry," Kade said, out of respect to his parents but not because he meant it.

"No problem. I like a person who speaks his mind."

The next day Dwight Allen returned to Chicago.

Two days before Christmas, just after supper, Kade's father came up to Kade's bedroom and suggested they do something together.

"Like what?"

"I don't know. Maybe a board game." He went to Kade's closet and looked up on the shelf where Kade kept his games. "How about Monopoly?"

Before Kade could react, his father had taken the Monopoly box down from the closet shelf. "I haven't played this for a long time." He sat on the bed and opened the box, then noticed the stack of drawings. "What's this?" he asked.

"Just some drawings I did," Kade said, his face turning bright red.

"Mind if I look at them?"

"No, I guess not."

His father looked at each drawing. "These are all of Brenda, aren't they?"

"Yes."

"Why so many of her?"

"I like the way she looks."

"I can tell you've spent a lot of time on these. They're very good." He paused. "Kade, how do you feel about Brenda?"

Kade's face felt like a furnace. "I love her."

"Does she know that?"

"Yeah, but she doesn't feel the same way about me because of the difference in our ages. She wants us to just be friends."

Kade was waiting to be lectured how wrong it was for him to feel the way he did about Brenda. Instead, his father turned wistful. "You know, when I was in junior high, I felt the same way about a girl in high school. She came twice a week to work in our school library. For a while there I checked out more books than anyone else in school. Sometimes five or six a day, just to watch her stamp the book and hand it back to me. She had the most beautiful red hair I've ever seen."

"Did you ever tell her how you felt?"

"I was too embarrassed to actually say it, so one time when I was returning a library book, I folded a love note into the checkout slip and handed the book to her. I knew she had to take the slip out and take a pencil and cross out the due date. I sat down at a nearby desk and waited. Just then the phone rang. Of all the rotten luck, it was for the girl. She went to take the call, and the head librarian, a crusty woman, came to the desk. She grabbed my book, removed the note, read it, and announced to the entire library, 'Who wrote this horrid note?' I got up and ran out of the library and never went back."

Kade smiled. "So it's not too awful to feel the way I do about Brenda?"

"Not as long as you can keep your feelings under control."

"Brenda makes sure of that. One time she told me she'd quit seeing me if I kept going on about how much

I liked her. So I don't talk about it much anymore. It's kind of hard sometimes, but I guess that's the way it's got to be. Sometimes I dream about her at night. It's a funny thing. In my dreams I'm always the same age as her." He paused. "Other than that, I've pretty much got it under control."

"It's not easy, is it," his dad said.

"No. I'm glad you told me about the girl with red hair."

"You suppose this runs in the family?" his dad said with a smile. He studied the drawings again. "These are exceptionally good. I think you should take art in school so you can develop this talent."

"They're not that good."

"Don't kid yourself. They're excellent."

"You really think so?"

"Absolutely."

"Thanks a lot. Dad, you won't tell Mom about this, will you?"

"Not if you don't want me to."

"I don't want her to worry."

"All right. I won't tell her."

"Thanks."

"I love you, Kade. Don't ever forget that—no matter what happens."

"I won't." It seemed an awkward moment. If Kade had been a little younger, he might have gone to his father for a hug, but now he held back. His father was likewise uncertain of what to do. It was new territory for both of them.

"You still want to play Monopoly?" his dad asked.

"Sure, if you do."

"Let's take this downstairs and see if we can talk your mother into playing with us."

"She always wins though," Kade said.

"This time she won't."

But sure enough, Denise won again.

On Christmas morning they gathered around the Christmas tree to open presents. Kade had a married sister, six years older than he, who lived in Orem, Utah. She sent him a BYU sweatshirt for Christmas. He also got two shirts and a pair of jeans and a watch and some underwear and a Levi jacket just like the one Brenda had and fifty dollars in cash, which could go toward him getting contact lenses. Now he was only thirty dollars from having enough to pay for the examination and lenses and also the insurance that his father insisted he get.

Even though he had received what he'd asked for, he felt a little disappointed there were no surprises. Christmas wasn't the same as it had been when he was little.

At about ten thirty Brenda and Emmet showed up. When Kade answered the door, Emmet smiled, as though he had a joke up his sleeve. "Can you help us? We need some help moving something that's kind of heavy."

"Sure, I can help."

"Come outside and let's get started."

Kade put on his boots and went outside. It was a cold, clear, sunny day, and the snow crunched under their feet. In the bed of Emmet's pickup was a set of homemade barbells, made from large gears from some old farm machinery. Every piece was painted a bright red.

"Oh, great! Barbells! This is just what I wanted!"

"Sure it is. You laid down enough hints," Emmet joked.

"No I didn't."

Emmet turned to Brenda. "Kade says to me, 'Either get me a set of barbells for Christmas or I'll start lifting Brenda over my head.' What was I to do? I knew if he tried that, it'd wreck his back for sure."

"Watch it there," Brenda playfully warned her father.

Kade touched the cold metal. "This is terrific! I can hardly wait to start working out."

"Where do you want us to take 'em?"

"How about up in my room?"

"Whatever you say. Brenda, you're in charge of opening and closing doors. Let's go."

Kade's mother was sitting at the kitchen table when the three of them burst into the house. Kade was the first one in, carrying two large red gears from some ancient machinery.

"Look what Emmet made me!" he called out.

"It's very nice," his mother said. "What is it?"

"A set of barbells."

Emmet was the next one in with a load. "Sorry for busting up your Christmas like this."

"Kade says you made him a set of barbells."

Emmet grinned. "Actually it was a way of getting rid of some of my junk."

Brenda was next. "Merry Christmas."

"Merry Christmas. It looks like you and your dad have made Kade's day."

"It was mostly Dad's idea."

The three of them were now up in Kade's room.

Paul came into the kitchen. "What's going on?" he asked.

"Emmet made Kade a set of barbells for Christmas. They just brought it over. Kade's really excited. You should've seen the look on his face just now. They've taken it all upstairs."

"Every time he sets the weights down, it'll jar the entire house. They should be put in the barn."

"I'd rather put up with a little noise than have him out in that cold barn."

"How can anyone make a set of barbells?" Paul asked.

Upstairs they heard Brenda. "Okay, Macho Man, show us your stuff." Pause. "All right! Look at that, would you? Dad, how many pounds is that?"

"Sixty," Emmet said.

"All right, Kade!"

The barbell crashed down onto the floor above them, making a terrible noise and causing a small piece of ceiling tile to fall down.

"If they keep this up, we're not going to have a ceiling," Paul complained.

A minute later there was another dull thud above their heads. And then Kade, Brenda, and Emmet bounded down the stairs.

"I'm going over to Brenda's," Kade said, grabbing his coat.

On his way out Emmet stopped to talk. "I hope this won't be too awful for you folks. Next time I come I'll bring an old carpet, and we'll lay a few layers on the floor so it won't be so noisy when Kade sets the weights down."

"We appreciate your taking time with Kade," Paul said.

"No problem. I always wanted to have a son, but I guess that wasn't in the cards. Kade's a good boy. You both should be very proud of him. Well, I'd better be going. We're going to try out a new video game I got for Brenda. Christmas is a great time of year, isn't it? Well, Merry Christmas."

"Merry Christmas," they answered back.

A minute later it was quiet again.

"It's hard to compete with that family," Paul said.

Denise shrugged. "That's what happens to kids. They grow up and pull away from their parents."

"I know that."

"Then what's the problem?" Denise asked.

"I don't know."

A few minutes later Kade called to see if he could

stay for lunch. Paul tried to persuade him not to, but Kade said they were having a big video-game tournament, and that if he left now, his team, composed of him and Brenda's mom, would have to forfeit.

"All right."

"Thanks, Dad. 'Bye."

Paul hung up. "Kade's staying over for lunch," he told Denise.

"Is that what you want him to do? This is Christmas, Paul. We can call him back if you want him here with us."

It was painful for him to say it. "I don't stack up very well alongside Emmet, do I?"

"What on earth are you talking about?"

"I mean as far as being the kind of a man a boy wants to spend time with."

"Paul, you're the most wonderful man I know. Someday Kade's going to realize that."

"Maybe so, but we're all in for some tough times real soon. I just hope Kade and I don't drift too far apart in the process."

"What are you talking about?"

Paul sighed. "This may be Emmet's last Christmas on the farm."

The visit by Dwight Allen had not been a social call. By the time he left Paul, they had agreed on a plan. Four farmers in the worst shape financially would be refused operating funds for the upcoming growing season. Dwight knew this might force some of the four to sell out altogether, but with the loans to each of these families being over 60 percent of equity, it would be irresponsible for the bank to continue to advance money to them.

"It's for the best," he told Paul just before getting on his chartered plane.

"Maybe so, but these are good people."

"Do you know them very well?"

"Two of them. Emmet Sloan and Harvey Mudlin."

"How do you know them?"

"The Sloans belong to our church, and the Mudlin boy is one of Kade's friends. Dwight, the thing that bothers me the most about all this is that it isn't entirely their fault."

Dwight shrugged. "Through the years I've noticed that most people who can't pay back their loans have good excuses. In this business, though, excuses don't count for much."

Paul shook his head.

"Something wrong?"

"I was just wondering what all this is going to do to my son."

Kade worked out every day after school. He liked to take his shirt off and look in the mirror for any sign that he was getting stronger. He got tired of tromping down the stairs all the time, so he asked his mother for a mirror in his room.

"What for?"

"So I can look at myself when I'm working out."

"Why on earth would you want to do that?"

"Mom, that's what weight lifters do."

"They must be very conceited then. I certainly don't want you to become like that."

"Oh, Mom," he grumbled.

Kade's birthday was the second week in January. His parents asked if he wanted a birthday party. He said all he wanted was to have Brenda over for cake and ice cream.

"Maybe you should spend with someone else besides Brenda all the time," his dad said.

"What for?"

"I just think it'd be for the best." He thought about it some more. "Oh, never mind. It's your birthday. You go ahead with whatever plans you want to make."

Brenda did come for birthday cake. She gave him a set of watercolor paints and a brush. His parents gave him a shirt, some cash toward the purchase of contact lenses, and a driver's training manual, which meant they'd decided to let him get a license.

"If you want, I can teach Kade how to drive," Brenda said.

"I thought that'd be something I'd do," his dad said.

"Kade'll probably learn real fast," Brenda said. She and Kade tried to keep from laughing.

"What's so funny?" his mother asked.

"Nothing."

After they had cake and ice cream, Kade took Brenda up to his room to watch him lift weights so she'd know how strong he was getting.

"Good job," she said as he lifted a barbell above his head.

He set the weights down. "I'm fifteen now and you're still sixteen," Kade said. "So there's only a year between us."

She smiled. "You think you're catching up with me, is that it?"

"It's not just age. It's everything else. My dad says I'm on a growth spurt. I'll be as tall as you are pretty soon. Stand up and turn around."

They stood back to back. She touched their heads with her hand. "No doubt about it, Kade, you're getting taller," she said.

"Anybody seeing us, like at a movie together, if they didn't know us, might never guess you're older than me."

"That's probably true."

"So I was wondering if you'd go out with me . . . " — he felt awkward saying it— ". . . on a date."

"Kade, c'mon, we've talked about this before."

"I know, but I'm older now."

"You've got me as a friend forever. Isn't that worth something?"

"I suppose."

"Okay then," she said. "Let's leave it at that." She paused. "Are you still drawing pictures of me?"

"Yes."

"Can I see them?"

He pulled down from the closet the box where he

kept her drawings and handed it to her. Then he sat on the floor next to the heater vent. She sat cross-legged on his bed and looked at the drawings.

Kade heard his mother coming up the stairs. Brenda quickly hid the box under the bed.

"Kade, I'm not sure you and Brenda should be up here all alone," his mother said.

"Why not?"

"A girl shouldn't be alone in a young man's bedroom."

"To Brenda this is more like babysitting than anything else."

"That's not true, Kade," Brenda said. "Your mom's probably right. Let's go downstairs."

"We'll be down in a minute," Kade said to his mother. She left.

Brenda looked through the stack of drawings. "You've got to let the art teacher in school see these."

"No."

"Why not?"

"What if she showed them to someone in her class?"

"What if she did?"

"Then everyone would know."

"Would know what?"

He looked away. "That I can't get you out of my mind."

"Look, I'm not so sure it's me. You're a natural-born artist. I think you'd be drawing pictures of any girl you spent as much time with as you do with me. I just happen to be around, that's all. The important thing is you can't just ignore a talent like this." She paused. "I've got an idea. What would you think if I took art with you next fall?"

He grinned. "The two of us in the same class? That'd be great."

"All right then, it's settled."

A week later the stake had a youth dance in Great Falls. Brenda asked Kade to ride with her. Melissa Simmons would have gone too, but she had to go visit her grandparents.

Winter had set in for good, but although it was cold and the countryside was covered with snow, the roads were clear and there was no wind.

Brenda let Kade drive the first little while. He liked being in the driver's seat with her beside him on their way to a dance.

"You think you're pretty hot stuff these days, don't you," she teased.

"What are you talking about?"

"I see you're wearing a short-sleeve shirt tonight. Is that so you can show off your muscles to all the girls?"

He was surprised she'd guessed.

"Let me see how strong your arms are now," she asked.

He gripped the steering wheel hard so his muscles would flex. She touched his upper arm. "It's coming along. I bet you set some girl's heart on fire tonight."

"At least one, maybe two," he said with a smile.

"You know what? I think I've created a monster."

"Who do you want to dance with tonight?" he asked.

"Hey, I'm not particular. Anybody who'll ask me."

"I'm serious."

"I don't know." She paused. "Jason Pasco maybe."

"What do you like about him?"

"He's fun to talk with, and he's got this really good sense of humor, and he's smart, and he tries to live the teachings of the Church." She paused. "And I like his looks . . . a lot."

"What do you like about his looks?"

"Well, he's got the most wonderful face. I don't know if you've noticed it before."

"Not really."

"What about you, Kade? Who do you want to dance with?"

"You."

"Who else?"

"Linda Cooper, I guess."

"Maybe this'll be our lucky night and Jason and Linda'll both be there," she said.

"Yeah, maybe so," he said quietly.

After they arrived at the stake center, they went in the cultural hall and looked around. There were pockets of kids clustered together, watching the braver ones out on the floor dancing.

"There's Linda," Brenda said. "Go ask her to dance."

"Not yet."

"Kade, come on. Don't be bashful."

"I want to stay with you."

"I'm not going to let you do that. Go dance with Linda."

"How about if you and I dance first, just so I'll get used to it."

"All right, one time, but then you have to promise to ask Linda."

"Okay."

He never wanted the dance to end. But it did.

"Now go ask Linda," she said.

"Just one more with you."

"No. C'mon, you promised."

"I'm as tall as you are now."

"That's because I have my shoes off. Go ask Linda."

"And I'm pretty sure I'm going to turn out taller and stronger and better looking than Jason. Especially once I get my contact lenses."

"Kade, I mean it now."

"Please. Just one more dance with you."

"No. Either you dance with Linda or I'm not talking to you anymore tonight."

He finally went and asked Linda to dance.

"You look different," Linda said while they danced.

"In what way?"

"I don't know. You seem more sure of yourself."

"Brenda's been helping me. You know what? The next time they have a stake dance, I'll be wearing contact lenses. I've pretty much got all my money saved. I'm pretty sure they'll make me look older." He glanced over at the sidelines. Jason was talking to Brenda. He watched them together. Things were going okay for her.

The two couples danced nearly every dance after that. Kade kept dancing with Linda because it was easier not to have to go find a new girl every time, and because she seemed to like him.

At eleven o'clock Jason and Brenda came over. "Jason wants to go out for something to eat. Linda, can you come too?"

"As long as we're back by midnight. That's when my mom is coming to pick me up."

"We'll be back by then. Kade and I have a two-hour drive ahead of us."

They had so much fun at McDonald's that they almost stayed too long. When they finally returned to the church parking lot, Linda's mother had already arrived and gone inside to look around. Linda said good night and left to find her mother.

A short time later Kade and Brenda were on the highway heading home.

"I had a good time tonight. What about you?" Brenda asked.

"It was okay."

"I think Linda is great for you."

"I suppose. Do you still like Jason?"

"Yes. Very much. He's a lot like you, except he's older."

"No kidding?"

"I wish I could somehow arrange for him to take me to our school's junior prom. I'm on the decorating committee. I'll be doing all this work on it, so if I possibly can, I want to go to it. But there's no chance anybody at school will ask me, seeing as how I've let it be known I don't want to have anything to do with drinking. And there's no guy in school my age who doesn't drink."

"Why don't you ask Jason to go with you?"

"He's supposed to ask me."

"But he lives so far away. He probably doesn't even know about the prom. If you want, I could phone and tell him about it."

"But what if he doesn't want to come all the way here just to go to a dance with me?"

"Then he won't ask you."

"I'd feel dumb knowing we sort of engineered the whole thing."

"Hey, don't worry. He'll want to take you."

"Well, okay, I guess it's all right if you phone Jason. As long as you do it on your own, and not because I told you to."

"Sure, no problem."

The next day Kade phoned Jason and told him about the junior prom.

"Hey, I'll take her. I'll call her up right now and ask her."

They hung up, and a few minutes later Brenda phoned and excitedly announced that Jason had just asked her to the prom.

On Monday at work Paul Ellis phoned Emmet Sloan. They talked about Kade and Brenda for a while and then Paul said, "I've been looking over your request for operating funds for this next year." He paused. "I was wondering if you and your wife could come in sometime soon so we could talk about it."

"What'd we do? Fill something in wrong again?" Emmet said. "Clayton Jones always used to just cross out my mistakes and write it in the way it was supposed to be."

"I just think it'd be best if we sat down and went over a few things."

"There's nothing wrong, is there?"

"I just think we need to go over a few things. When will you and Susan be in town next?"

"We can come in anytime. When's a good time for you?"

"How about tomorrow morning, say, at eleven o'clock?"

"Sounds good. I'll see you then."

After school that same day, Brenda asked Kade if he'd mind if they stopped at a local dress shop before going home, while she looked for a prom dress.

A few minutes later, in the store, Kade sat in a chair as Brenda came out wearing a low-cut formal.

"What do you think about this one?" she asked.

"Shows too much," he said, then started to blush.

She looked in the mirror. "Gosh, you're right. Sorry."

Soon she came out in another dress. "What about this one?"

"It's better."

"It's the most expensive one."

"How much is it?"

She showed him the price tag. He couldn't believe one dress could cost so much.

"There's another one that isn't as much. I'll go try that one on."

In a few minutes she was back out again, wearing a pastel pink formal. "Well?"

"That's the best one. I really like that color on you."

"I like it too. Well, I think I'll look around a little more, but if I can't find anything better, I'll probably get this one."

Tuesday at eleven Emmet and Susan Sloan showed up at the bank for their appointment.

"Can I get you two anything?" Paul asked. "Some hot chocolate maybe?"

"No thanks. Let's get this taken care of first. I've had such bad luck filling out forms that I've taken to letting Susan do it. She doesn't make many mistakes, but apparently she did this time."

"Actually, the form was filled out correctly."

"Then what's the problem?" Emmet asked.

Paul turned to some figures he'd written down. "I've looked at your overall credit situation. Emmet, your outstanding loans now total 60 percent of equity. We red-flag anything over 50 percent as being in trouble."

"Except for our operating loan, we haven't taken out any new loans the past year," Susan said.

"The problem is that land values have dropped so drastically. Take a case of someone with loans totaling forty-five percent of equity. What happens if the price of land drops to half of what it was? Now that person's loans are ninety percent of equity. A bank can't tolerate that because it becomes doubtful the loan can ever be repaid. Your situation isn't that serious, but it's bad enough that you ought to be thinking of ways to reduce your indebtedness."

"If we're in trouble," Emmet said, "then you people are the ones to blame. Every year Clayton Jones came out and suggested improvements we could make—just so he could loan us some more money."

"Clayton didn't always use his head when it came to making loans."

"And you do?" Susan countered.

"One of the reasons I was sent here was to try and improve the bank's financial situation."

"Are there other people around here in the same boat as me?" Emmet asked.

"Yes."

"Who are they?"

"I can't tell you that."

Susan came to her husband's defense. "Paul, ask anyone and they'll tell you Emmet runs the best operation in this country. Two years ago he was chosen as the county's outstanding farmer."

"I know that."

"So how can you tell him he's suddenly in trouble?"

"What's happened isn't his fault. We base everything on the price of land, and it's dropped a lot lately."

"You must have called us in here for a reason. What is it?" Emmet asked.

"You asked for a larger limit on your operating loan. I'm afraid I can't give you that."

"What are we supposed to do then?" Susan said. "We need money to produce a crop."

"You might lease out your land to someone else, or if worse comes to worst, you could sell off some of your land."

"But you just said the price of land is low," Emmet said. "This'd be the absolute worst time to sell."

"I realize that."

"We can do business with someone else, that's what we can do," Emmet said.

"That's up to you."

"They don't make bankers like they used to, do they," Emmet commented. "At least Clayton Jones had a heart. He knew farming and he believed in the people around here." He shook his head. "I don't go to church much, but Susan is one of the most faithful members you've got. You're her branch president. And so to reward her faithfulness, you're going to refuse us a loan?"

"I have a responsibility to the bank's best interests. You may not believe it, but also I'm doing this for your good too."

"There's one thing I don't understand."

"What's that?"

"How did someone like you produce such a good kid as Kade?" Emmet turned on his heels and walked out.

Susan lingered. "I don't understand this. I thought we were friends. Why are you turning against us?"

"I'm not turning against you. I'm trying to help you both see you've got to make some changes or else you might lose everything."

"I can't believe this is happening to us."

"I'm sorry I had to be the one to tell you."

She left and went out to join Emmet in the pickup. Paul watched them go and then asked his secretary not to disturb him for a while. He closed the door to his office and sat at his desk, his head cupped in his hands.

He had three more farmers to see that day.

The next day after school, Brenda went back with Kade to try on the formal she'd liked the day before.

"I still like this one," she said. "How about you?"

"Yeah. You look great in it."

"I guess I'll take it then."

"How are you going to pay for it?" he asked.

"I've got some money in the bank. And my dad owes me for some work I did for him. It'll all work out."

"Can we go now?" he asked.

"Sure. I'll go change."

The clerk finished up with another customer and then came over to where Kade was sitting. "What did she decide?"

"She decided to buy it."

"Good. I think she looks real nice in it, don't you?"

"She always looks nice."

"Are you the lucky guy who's taking her to the prom?"

"Me? No, I'm just a tag-along."

"Don't believe that," Brenda called out from the dressing room. "Kade's my best friend."

"Who's she going to the prom with?" the clerk asked Kade.

"You wouldn't know him. He's from Great Falls."

"Well, he'll be pleased how nice she'll look in that formal."

"Yes, he will."

Brenda came out of the dressing room carrying the formal. "Can you hold this for a couple of days until I have the money to pay for it?"

"Sure, no problem."

Kade had never seen Brenda so happy. She let him drive. She had him stop at the drive-in and bought them both some hot chocolate, and she talked him into singing along with her to the songs on the radio. He knew that when he got home he would draw a picture of the way she looked, so happy and alive and full of hope.

That night at nine o'clock Brenda phoned him. She sounded upset. "I need to talk to you right away."

"What's wrong?"

"Everything. I'll come and pick you up, okay?"

"Sure."

He went downstairs and put on his coat and waited for Brenda.

"Where do you think you're going?" his mother asked.

"Brenda needs someone to talk to."

"No you don't, young man. This is a school night, and you need your sleep."

"Mom, Brenda needs me. She was practically crying when she talked to me on the phone."

"You talk to your father about leaving."

Paul came into the kitchen. "What's the problem?"

"Kade says he's going out to talk to Brenda. I told him tonight's a school night and he should be going to bed now. He wouldn't listen to me. Paul, you talk to him."

"I think we'd better let him go."

"Why are you taking his side?"

"I think Brenda probably needs someone to talk to."

"I don't understand you at all sometimes, Paul." She turned to Kade. "Don't blame me if you get sick because you don't get enough sleep at night."

Kade saw headlights sweep across the yard. He said goodbye and hurried out so he'd be there when Brenda arrived.

A minute later they were driving toward town.

"What's wrong?" Kade asked.

"Didn't your dad tell you?"

"What?"

"He refused to loan us any more money. Kade, we've got to have operating funds. If we don't get any, we won't be able to farm this summer, so we might end up losing everything."

"There must be some mistake. My dad wouldn't do that."

"I'm not making this up."

"What are you going to do?"

"My dad's going to see if he can find someplace else to get the money." She paused. "We'll just have to wait. One thing for sure. I can't go to the prom now."

"You've got to go. Jason's expecting you."

"How can I? It costs too much money. For all I know, we might end up needing every penny for food."

"Don't call Jason yet about not going."

"Why?"

"Something might turn up."

"What?"

"I don't know. Just hold off before you call him, okay?"

"Okay, but it won't do any good."

They drove in silence for a while and then she said, "I'm sorry it had to be your dad. I think this might make it harder for you and me to be friends."

"We can't let it do that."

She nodded. "I agree. I'd miss having you around to talk to."

They stopped at a cafe and had something to eat and then drove back. It was nearly eleven before Kade walked in the door. He thought his parents were asleep, but as he went into the kitchen he saw his dad. "How's Brenda doing?" he asked Kade.

"Not very good. Is it true what she said about you not loaning them the money they need?"

"Yes, it's true. I can't talk about my reasons. You'll just have to trust that I'm trying to do what's best for them."

"They don't look at it that way."

"I know that."

"How can you do that to a family that belongs to the Church?"

"I have to think of what's best for the bank."

"You don't care what happens to them, do you." Kade's comment was a statement, not a question.

His father sighed, then said, "It's because I do care about them that I'm doing what I'm doing."

Kade looked at him. "I hope I never get to be like you," he said, then went upstairs to his room.

He had just put on his pajamas when his dad appeared at the top of the stairs. "Kade, we need to talk."

They sat down on the bed. "Where do you suppose the money comes from that a bank loans?" Paul asked.

"I don't know."

"In our bank we have the life savings of other farmers in the area. Parents put a few dollars a month into an account for their children's education. Young married couples save for a down payment for their first home. We even have the money you're saving for contact lenses. People trust us with their savings. Don't I have a responsibility to them to make sure their money is safe?"

"I guess so."

Paul stood up. "Well, we'd both better get to bed. It's been a tough day. Do you want me to get the light?"

"Yes, please."

"Good night."

"Good night, Dad."

At school the next morning Kade couldn't stop thinking about Brenda. At nine o'clock he decided he was wasting his time being in class. He left school and walked down to the bank. His dad's car wasn't there, so he went in and withdrew all the money he'd been saving for contact lenses. Then he went to the store where Brenda had picked out a formal.

"What can I do for you?" the clerk asked.

"Brenda Sloan and I were in here yesterday. She had you set aside a formal. I'm here to pay for it."

"Does she know you're doing this?"

"No, it's sort of a surprise." Kade pulled out a roll of bills from his front pocket.

"I'll go get it. Will you be taking it with you now?"

"Yes."

"Will she need a slip or some shoes?"

Kade paused. "She's probably got all that stuff already."

After he paid for the formal, Kade said, "There's just one other thing. The formal is my gift to her, but she might try to return it. If she does, do me a favor and tell her you can't take it back, okay?"

"Why are you doing this?"

"Because she's my friend."

"Why can't she pay for it herself?"

"Her dad's a farmer, and they're going through tough times."

The woman, born and raised in the area, understood.

Kade walked back to school. He put the formal in the pickup, then returned to class.

After school, by the time he made it to the pickup, Brenda was already there looking at the formal.

He climbed in the pickup. "What's that?" he asked.

"It's the formal I picked out. Why is it here?"

"I don't know. Maybe the Prom Elf brought it."

"You did it, didn't you?"

"Me? Do I look like a Prom Elf?"

"I can't let you do it. I'm taking it back right now."

"They won't take it back."

"How do you know?"

"Remember the woman who waited on us the other day? While you were changing, she told me it's their policy. Look, go back to the store and find out for yourself if you don't believe me."

"Kade, where'd you get the money to pay for it?"

"The Prom Elf doesn't need money."

"Was it from the money you've been saving for contacts?"

"You're talking to the wrong person. You should be talking to the Prom Elf."

"You've been saving for so long for contacts. It isn't right for you to do this."

"I'll tell you what's not right. It's not right that your dad should be refused a loan."

"My parents will never let me keep this when they find out you paid for it. We don't take charity."

"Tell them you picked it up at the Salvation Army for a couple of bucks."

"They wouldn't believe that."

"Why not?"

"Kade, you can't pick up a brand-new formal at the Salvation Army."

"Mess it up a little then."

"That'd be deceiving my parents."

"Maybe so, but it'd get you to the prom. Brenda, I'm serious, the store won't take the formal back. So what do you want to do, hang it in your closet or wear it to the prom?"

She thought about it for a long time. "All right, I'll go."

On the way home he folded the dress into a ball and sat on it so it wouldn't look brand new when she showed it to her mother.

"What about your contact lenses?" she asked.

"They probably wouldn't have made me look older anyway."

"You truly are the nicest guy I've ever known in my whole life."

He smiled. "It wasn't me. It was the Prom Elf. Every year the Prom Elf looks for the most beautiful, deserving girl in all the world. This year it just happened to be you."

"Kade," she said, her voice wavering, "I'll never forget this, not if I live to be a hundred."

"Me neither," he said.

The next day at school Marvin Mudlin came up to Kade, his face red with anger. "Tell your dad thanks for everything."

"I'm sorry."

"I try to be friends with you and look what it gets me." With that, Marvin left him.

The few days before the prom were a blur of activity. Together, Kade and Brenda planned every detail.

"Where do you think Jason and I should eat before the prom?"

"Pat's Diner."

"You can't eat there for a prom. It's too ordinary."

"So what? Everything in this town is ordinary." He paused. "You might try the Dixie Inn. I ate there once. It was all right. By the way, where's Jason going to stay when you two finally call it a night?"

"He'll stay at Sister Simmons's."

"Great. That'll make Melissa happy."

"Are you going to start on Melissa?" she asked.

"She's such a witch sometimes. How can someone as nice as Sister Simmons have a daughter like her?"

"She'll grow up one of these days."

"Sure, in about fifty years."

"Kade, don't be so negative all the time."

"I'm sorry, but it's what males do when they develop sexually. They exhibit aggressive characteristics."

Brenda burst out laughing.

"It's true," Kade said. "I read it in the barber shop when I was getting a haircut. Of course, it was about mule deer, but I think the same thing applies to a guy."

"You're so funny sometimes."

"Hey, maybe I wasn't trying to be funny. Did you ever think of that?"

"Oh, gosh, Kade, we have such good times together, don't we?"

"Yeah, that's for sure."

"In a way I wish you could come with Jason and me to the prom."

"I'm sure he wouldn't mind if I sat between you two in the car."

"Why not? I bet the three of us'd have a good time."

"Except when he tried to kiss you."

"Maybe he won't try."

"If he does, are you going to let him?"

She paused. "I don't know. What do you think?"

He thought about it. "I'd say go ahead."

She was surprised. "Really? Why?"

"Because he's laying out a lot of money, and I think he should get something back in return."

"You're awful, you know that?" she said.

"What's awful?"

"I won't kiss a guy just because he's put out money for a date."

"Why not?"

"Because when two people kiss, it's supposed to mean they really like each other."

"Well, you do what you want, but he's going to figure it's a big waste if you don't kiss him at least once."

"How do you know that?"

"I just do."

"You're only fifteen."

"I listen to guys talk in the locker room."

"Jason's not like those guys."

"Maybe not, but he has some of the same male characteristics."

She smiled. "Are you going to talk about mule deer again?"

"I say give the guy a good-night kiss."

"Well, I don't know. I'll think about it."

"Good."

They were in front of his house. "Thanks for the ride," he said.

"Sure. See you tomorrow."

On Saturday, the day of the prom, Brenda asked him over while her mother fixed her hair. When he got there, they were in the kitchen. He sat down and they talked. Emmet came in a while later.

"Come and take a look at your daughter, Emmet."

He took one look and smiled. "You look like a creature from outer space with those rollers in your hair."

"Thanks, Dad," she said. "That really builds my confidence."

"Are you fishing for a compliment? The best thing you've got going for you is that you've got your mother's beauty." He noticed Kade. "Hi, Kade. How's it going? What are you doing, making sure they do it right?"

"Something like that." He paused. "I'm sorry about my dad not loaning you the money you need."

"Don't worry about it. We're working on getting another loan. Things'll work out."

"Speaking of that, Otis Cramer called," Susan said.

"What did he want?"

"He wanted to know when was a good time to come out and look around and help us fill out a loan application."

"Tell him to come anytime it's convenient for him." He looked at the clock on the wall. "Well, I'd better be going."

"Daddy, will you be around at five when Jason comes to pick me up?"

He smiled. "You bet. I thought that'd be a good time to clean my shotgun. Just to let him know what'll happen if he doesn't treat you right."

Brenda laughed. "You would, too, wouldn't you!"

"You bet I would."

"Well, if you promise not to do that, I'll let you see what the finished product looks like. Just so you'll know you really do have a daughter here."

"No kidding? Is that what you are? No wonder you look different in jeans than I do."

She grinned. "Sure. For one thing I don't have a big paunch around my middle like some people I could name."

"Watch it," Emmet said. "You're getting into deep waters now." He glanced at Kade. "Kade, you ever wish you were Brenda's age?"

"Daddy," Brenda objected.

"All the time," Kade said.

"Well, if it's any consolation, age isn't that important once you're out of high school. A lot of people don't know this, but Susan here is five years older than me."

"Such lies," Susan said. "You'll never get anybody to believe that."

"Kade here believes it. Don't you, Kade?"

"Sure. If you said it, it must be true."

"You see there? Kade and me, we stick together. Well, I gotta run."

"Where are you going?" Susan asked.

"Into town. A few of us are getting together at the diner to talk about our options. He looked at Kade. "You probably never figured a dumb farmer like me would use the word options, did you? It's what happens when your back is up against the wall."

After Emmet left, Kade got up to leave. Brenda invited him back at four thirty. "You can see me all fixed up and glamorous."

"I'm going over to Brenda's," Kade said a little before four thirty.

"What for?" his mother asked.

"To see Brenda with her formal on."

"Are you sure they want you over there now?"

"Brenda invited me."

"All right."

"Can I use the car?"

"When will you be back?"

"I don't know. I don't think I'll be very long."

"Your father will be home in an hour."

"Where is he?"

"At his office." She paused. "Kade, he's going through a tough time right now. If you could . . . "

"What?"

"If you could just try and see things from his point of view."

"Mom, he's refusing to loan money to Brenda's father and Mr. Mudlin. It's not fair. They need money to keep things going until their crops get harvested."

"There's some things you don't know. You'll just have to trust that your father is trying to do the right thing."

He sighed. "I just don't see why he has to be so strict all the time."

"Kade, this is a difficult time for everyone, including your father."

A few minutes later Kade sat at the kitchen table in Brenda's home and waited. Her mother came into the room. "Ladies and gentlemen, may I present the most enchanting young woman in the entire world."

Brenda appeared, ready for the prom. Besides being embarrassed that her mother was making such a fuss over her, she radiated something else. It was the realization that somehow in the process of growing up, she had become a beautiful woman.

"What do you think?" she asked.

"Wow," he said softly. "You look great."

"Thank you," she said somewhat formally, not sounding like the girl in jeans he rode to school with every day.

They heard a door slam. Emmet walked in, took one look at Brenda, and stopped in his tracks. "Gosh, gal, you ought to get gussied up more often."

"I couldn't work outside with you if I did that. You still think I should?"

"You got me there all right." He turned to Kade. "We're interested in knowing what a typical teenage boy thinks of the way my daughter looks."

"She's the best-looking girl I've ever seen."

Emmet nodded. "And there you have it, folks."

"Let me get a picture of Brenda and Kade together," Susan said.

"No, not me," Kade objected.

"Oh, sure. Don't go shy on us now. Stand alongside Brenda. Emmet, you get in there too."

Brenda was in the middle with Kade on her left and Emmet on her right. "Talk about your rose among thorns," Brenda said.

"Kade and me think it's the thorn among roses. Right, Kade?"

"You bet."

"And besides, Missy, you're not so dolled up you can't be tickled."

There was a quiet elegance in her bearing that allowed her to take charge. "Not tonight," she said. That was all it took.

"I'm going to go make some punch for when Jason comes," Susan said.

"Dad, you behave yourself when Jason comes, okay?"

"All right, if I have to. Well, I do need to get on the horn and talk to a few people. Come and get me when he shows up. I have a list of one hundred rules I want to read to him before he takes you out."

Kade and Brenda went to the living room and sat down.

"You're kind of quiet tonight," she said.

"Yeah, I guess I am. You look so different."

"I feel different."

"How do you mean?"

"I feel more like a woman."

"Guys who see you at the dance are going to get weak in the knees, and if you happen to smile at them, they won't be able to sleep tonight. Girls are going to hate you because you look better than they do. And Jason is going to feel like he's taking out Miss America."

"And to think I owe it all to the Prom Elf."

He shrugged. "It wasn't that big of a deal."

"Kade, in some ways I wish I were going to the prom with you."

"Me? Why?"

"Because you're the best friend I ever had."

They heard a car pull into the driveway. "That must be Jason," she said.

A few minutes later Jason and Brenda left for the restaurant.

"I'd better be going now," Kade said.

"We thought we'd peek in tonight and see how the dance is going," Emmet said. "You want to ride into town with us about nine?"

"Okay."

Kade went home and ate supper and watched TV until eight thirty and then went to his dad, who was preparing the lesson he would give in priesthood meeting. "Brenda's parents invited me to go into town with them to watch Brenda and Jason dance."

"Are you all ready for church tomorrow?" he asked.

"Pretty much."

"Have you taken a shower and washed your hair?"

"I'll do that in the morning."

"All right. Don't stay out too late."

When they arrived at the school, they went up to the bleachers, where they could look down on the dance-floor without being seen. Jason and Brenda were dancing. They looked good together.

"Our baby is growing up," Susan said.

"And I'm losing the best farmhand I've ever had," Emmet said. He paused and then added, "In fact, I might even be losing the farm."

"Let's forget all that tonight," Susan said.

After watching for a few minutes, they left. "What do you say we stop at the diner and see if anybody's there?" Emmet said.

"You men must spend half your waking life in that place."

"That's our office. Kade, you want a dish of ice cream, don't you?"

"Sure."

"I thought so."

They walked in and sat down in a booth. The waitress came over. "Mary Ellen, what's a good-looking girl like you doing here when you could be over at the dance?"

"You mean the high school dance? Emmet, I'm twenty-nine years old."

"You are? Gosh, you could've fooled me. You look a lot younger than that."

She smiled. "You're just saying that because you want an extra-large piece of pie. Well, you've outdone yourself this time, Emmet. For that compliment I might just give you the whole pie."

Emmet seemed to know everyone who walked in. He'd call out a greeting, and people would come over and talk.

A man and his wife entered the diner and saw Emmet and Susan. They came over, pulled up some chairs, and sat down.

"Emmet, I hear you're in the same boat as me," the man said.

"Yeah, that's right."

"If that idiot over at the bank thinks he can just shut us down, he's got another think coming."

Emmet cleared his throat. "This is Kade. He's Paul Ellis's son."

"Sorry, Kade, but it doesn't change the way I feel. We're not going to put up with the treatment we've been getting from the bank lately."

"I hope you come out on top," Kade said.

"The kid's got more sense than his old man," the man said.

"We'd better go," Susan said to Emmet.

"Yeah, I guess we'd better. We need to get Kade home. You two, don't be strangers. Drop over sometime and we'll play cards like we used to."

"Maybe we will," the man said, "if you promise not to cheat like you usually do."

"Hey, you're the one who taught me how to play the game," Emmet said.

Later that night Kade was awakened when he heard a vehicle coming down the lane. It stopped in front of the house, and a minute later he heard Brenda under his window calling his name. He opened the window and leaned out.

"Kade, I want to talk to you."

He got dressed and went outside and got into the pickup with Brenda.

"I just got home from the dance," she said.

"What time is it?"

"One o'clock."

"How was it?"

"It was the most wonderful night of my life."

"Did you give Jason a good-night kiss?"

"Yes."

"That's nice. For him, I mean."

She smiled. "For me too."

"No kidding?"

"I really like him."

"I'm glad."

"I saved the last dance for you because of what you did to make it so I could go to the prom. Let's go into the barn where it's dry."

She didn't have boots, so he carried her through the snow to the barn. He flipped on the light. The barn was cold and barren. She removed her coat, leaving her bare shoulders exposed to the cold.

"Are you sure you want to do that?" he said. "It's really freezing in here."

"I'll be okay. Dance with me, Kade."

She hummed a song as they danced. There were tears in her eyes. He thought about holding her close to him to try and keep her warm, but he wasn't sure if he should do that or not. Before he could decide, she quit dancing. "Kade, I'll never ever forget what you did for me." She kissed him on the cheek, then turned and reached for her coat and put it on.

He carried her back to the pickup. A minute later she left, and he went inside and went to bed. He couldn't sleep for a long time, though; he could still smell the fragrance of her perfume.

At seven that morning his father came to the foot of the stairs and called for Kade to get up and get ready for church.

The family arrived at the Odd Fellows Hall at eight thirty and started cleaning up, so that by a quarter to nine they were ready to begin. Attendance was way down that Sunday. The people assigned to give talks weren't there. The deacon assigned to bring bread had also not shown up, so Kade was sent out at the last minute to a store to buy some. By the time he returned, it was ten minutes after nine—and yet there was still hardly anyone there.

Kade's father got up to conduct the meeting. "I guess our speakers haven't shown up yet."

"The Aldriches said they weren't coming anymore as long as you were branch president," one of the older women said. "They said they can't see how you can be a branch president and refuse hard-working people loans to run their farms."

Kade wasn't sure if his father would be able to carry on with the meeting. A minute passed. The Simmons's baby began crying, and Sister Simmons took her out to the kitchen.

Finally his father spoke. "I never asked to be branch president." He stopped. "I'm sorry. You didn't come to hear that—you came to partake of the sacrament. Let's at least do that today."

Kade was painfully aware that Jason and Brenda were there. He wondered if Jason would go home and tell everyone how awful church was in Shelby.

After the sacrament, his father stood up again. "Our speakers still haven't shown up. Are there any volunteers?"

"I have a poem I could read," Sister Richardson volunteered.

"Please, that would be wonderful."

She read the poem and then rambled on for about ten minutes. A couple of other people got up and bore their testimonies. And then the meeting ended. Because there were so few people there, the Sunday School classes had to be combined.

After they got home from church, Kade's dad tried to get hold of the stake presidency, but he was told they were traveling to another ward that day and wouldn't be home until much later.

Kade had wanted to go over and see Brenda in the afternoon, but she had told him at church that she was probably going to sleep most of the day, and so he went up to his room and sketched out what it had been like when they danced in the cold and empty barn. With just one overhead light on, the darkness and shadows and harsh cold provided marked contrast to her warmth and beauty.

Around four in the afternoon the phone rang. Kade's father took the call on the kitchen phone. Kade was having a snack, so he could hear his father's end of the conversation.

" . . . President Mathesen, thanks for returning my call . . . You know I work for the bank here in town. I'm sure you're aware the farm economy is in a real slump these days. I've had to refuse loaning any more money to some of the farmers in the area until they do something to improve their financial situation. Well, the word's gotten out. Some of our members are staying away from church because of my being the branch president . . . Well, I'm thinking I might be the wrong man for this calling . . . Maybe if I had counselors, it'd be different . . . No, there's nobody who could be a counselor . . . I have prayed, President. There's nobody . . . All right, I'll try fasting about it too. President

Mathesen, you've got to come up here and see if you need to release me . . . Yes, next Sunday would be great. Thank you. Goodbye." He hung up the phone. "Kade?"

"Yes."

"Get your mother. I'd like to have family council."

A minute later the three of them, sitting around the kitchen table, began family council. Kade was asked to give the prayer.

His father seemed off balance and somber. "I talked to President Mathesen. He'll be visiting our branch next Sunday. I thought I'd fast and pray for help, and I was wondering if my family would be willing to join me."

"Of course we will," his mother answered. "When?"

"We could start after our evening meal today and go until our evening meal tomorrow."

"I have school tomorrow," Kade said.

"If you'd rather not fast, that's all right," his dad said.

"Kade," his mother said, "this is really important to your father."

"I don't like to fast."

"He doesn't have to if he doesn't want to," his father said.

His mother put her hand on Kade's arm. "Won't you do this one thing for your father?"

The way she said it made him feel guilty. "All right." He paused. "Can we pray for Emmet and for Marvin Mudlin's dad and all the others too?"

"Yes, of course," his dad said.

For supper they had split pea soup and tuna sandwiches. Then they went into the living room and knelt down. His dad offered the prayer as they began their fast.

That night Brenda invited him over to study with her. The minute he walked in her house, he knew he was in trouble because of the smell of cinnamon rolls baking in the oven.

After he'd been there for half an hour, Emmet invited Brenda and Kade to the kitchen for a snack.

"I can't eat," Kade said.

"Why not?"

"I'm fasting."

"What for?" Emmet asked.

"Our family is doing it because of my dad. Things aren't going very well for him these days, both at the bank and at church. So we're fasting so he'll know what to do, and also for the farmers in trouble."

Emmet looked at the platter of cinnamon rolls. "Susan, let's have these some other time. It wouldn't be fair for us to eat in front of Kade."

"Does that mean we'll be fasting too?" Susan asked.

Emmet paused. "I guess it does."

"And praying?" Susan said.

Emmet cleared his throat. "I suppose you got to have one with the other, don't you?"

"Yes," Susan said.

"All right, we'll pray too." He turned to Susan. "I'm kind of new at this. You got any suggestions?"

"I think it'd be nice to have family prayer."

"All right."

"Maybe if we knelt down too," Susan said.

Emmet got out of his chair and knelt down.

"We've never prayed before as a family," Brenda said as she and Kade knelt down.

"There's always the first time. Now what?" Emmet asked Susan.

"I think it'd be nice if you said the prayer."

"Me?"

"You're the head of this family."

"But I don't even go to church."

"You're still the head of the family."

"I think you should start going to church," Kade said.

"Why?"

"My dad needs help in church too."

"He and I are on opposite sides these days. It wouldn't make much sense for the two of us to be in church together, would it?"

"Maybe it'd help," Brenda said.

"How?"

"I don't know."

"Me neither. Well, I guess we'd better pray," Emmet's prayer came painfully slow, but he did it.

When Kade got home his mother had gone to bed. His father was in his office, sitting at his desk, reading the scriptures. Kade went in to see him. His father looked up from his reading. "You're home."

"Yes."

"You'd better get to bed so you'll get your rest."

"All right."

His father read for a few seconds and then, not hearing the sound of Kade's footsteps, turned around. "Is anything wrong?"

"No." Kade wanted to do something that would let his dad know what was in his heart. Without knowing exactly why he did it, he went over and put his hand on his dad's shoulder. The two of them froze in place, neither one wanting the experience to end, both hesitant to ask why this gesture of affection was there when it had been absent between them for so long.

"Dad?"

"Yes."

"I know this is a hard time for you. I hope everything turns out okay."

A long time passed, and then his father, his voice husky with emotion, said, "Thank you. I appreciate that."

Kade removed his hand from his father's shoulder. "I guess I'll go to bed now."

"All right. Good night, son."

"Good night, Dad."

The next morning his mother was sitting at the kitchen table when he passed by on his way out of the house to go to seminary. "Kade, you don't have to fast all day if it gets to be too hard. If you feel sick or anything, be sure and have something to eat."

"I will."

"Your father appreciates what you said to him last night."

"Oh."

"I packed you a snack just in case you need it during the day."

"I won't need it."

"It won't hurt to take it along, just in case."

Brenda pulled into the driveway. He took the sack of food his mother had fixed him and left.

As they were pulling onto the county road, he said, "My mom packed a snack in case I decided I need to eat, and so you can have it too, if you need it."

"Do you think you'll need it?" she asked.

"No."

"Have you ever fasted before on a weekday?" she asked.

"No."

"Me neither. Could we get together at lunchtime and go to the library?" she asked.

"Sure."

At lunch they went to the library and talked. It was the first time she'd ever openly associated with him at school. There was an unspoken rule against a junior girl choosing a freshman boy as a friend. But on that day she didn't seem to care. They sat where anybody who came into the library could see them. Once she even put her hand on his arm and left it there for several seconds.

Marvin Mudlin saw them together. He probably would have walked by, but Kade made the first move. "Hi, Marvin."

He stopped. "Hey, Kade, what's this? You chasing older women these days?"

"We're just studying together."

"I don't see why Brenda spends time with you when I'm available."

Kade smiled. "What can I say? Some guys got it and some don't."

Their joking was an uphill battle. It was followed by an awkward silence.

"How's your dad getting along?" Kade finally asked.

"Okay. Right now he's trying to find some other place to get a loan."

"Look, you guys," Kade said, "I'm really sorry about all this."

"We know you are," Brenda said.

Marvin sat down at the table. "Brenda, did you ever hear about the time Kade defended your honor?"

"No. When was that?"

"Just after you broke up with Doug. We were in the locker room after practice, and Doug started mouthing off about his dates with you. We all knew he was lying, but for some reason we let him go on anyway. Except for Kade. He told Doug to shut up. They were just about to fight when I grabbed Doug and made him take back the things he was saying."

"Thanks, Marvin. I'm glad Kade didn't have to fight Doug."

"I should've been the one to tell Doug to quit. I knew he was lying, but I let him go on anyway. Kade was the one who first stepped in. That really impressed me." He paused. "Well, I'd better be going."

After Marvin left, Kade tried to study, but he was

aware that Brenda was staring at him. "What?" he finally asked.

"What am I ever going to do with you?"

"I don't know."

"I don't know either."

That evening before supper, Kade's family had family prayer. After it was over, his father said, "I have an answer about what to do."

"Tell us," Kade said.

"You'll have to wait until Sunday to find out."

On Tuesday night, while Kade was studying, his mother came upstairs. "President Mathesen is going to come and stay with us Saturday night. Would it be okay if we gave him your room and had you sleep on the couch in the living room?"

"Will I have to clean my room?"

"Yes, of course. Kade, it'll be so good for your dad to have President Mathesen here. Can I count on you to help me get ready for him?"

"Okay."

Kade cleaned his room on Saturday morning. As he straightened out his desk, he came across a copy of *Time* that he'd been keeping for a long time. It contained a painting done by a famous artist of a scantily clad woman. Shortly after the magazine had come in the mail, Kade had taken it upstairs to see if he could draw a picture of the woman the way she was in the magazine. While he worked on it, his dad called him down for family prayer. To make matters worse, he was asked to say the prayer. Afterwards he returned to his room and looked at what he had drawn. He felt like a hypocrite. He crumpled up the drawing and promised himself he

123

wouldn't draw any more pictures like that. He crumpled up the paper and took it to school the next morning and dropped it in one of the large wastepaper baskets in the hall. Even if somebody found it, nobody would know that he was the one who had done the drawing.

That seemed like a long time ago. Kade had been true to the promise he'd made himself—but still he kept the magazine in his room. And sometimes he even looked at the picture. Now, knowing that President Mathesen would be staying in his room, he decided it was a good time to get rid of that temptation. He carried the magazine out to the trash incinerator.

Later that day he tried to think if there was anything else in his life that needed throwing out. He wondered what it would be like if the Savior was going to spend the night in his room. What things in his life would he change then? He went inside himself to find the weaknesses he needed to overcome, so that by the time the room was done, he felt clean too.

President Mathesen arrived at about eight o'clock on Saturday night.

"President, Kade will show you up to your room," his mother said. "Be sure and watch your head on the stairs."

Kade led him up the stairs to his room. "This is it."

"I'm sorry to be bumping you out of your room."

"No problem."

"Do you always keep it this clean?"

Kade smiled. "No."

"Good. My sons will be glad to hear that. They hate to be told about boys who keep their rooms clean."

At nine that night Kade took a shower and washed his hair because his mother said they had to leave President Mathesen as much time in the bathroom as he needed in the morning. After Kade's shower, he changed into a pair of pajamas, rolled out his sleeping bag on the couch, shut the door, and turned the TV on low so it wouldn't disturb anyone.

A little while later the doorbell rang. His mother opened the door, and he heard the voices of Brenda's parents and then Brenda herself. His mother took them into the kitchen, and Kade heard President Mathesen greeting them. "I'll need to talk to Brother Sloan alone if I might," President Matheson said.

Suddenly the door to the living room opened and the light went on. Brenda and the two mothers were standing in the doorway.

"Oh, gosh, I forgot about Kade being in here," his mother said.

"It's all right, Mom. I'm not asleep."

They came in. Still in his sleeping bag, he sat up on the couch.

"Hi," he said to Brenda.

"Hi." She sat down in a chair next to the couch.

"How was President Mathesen's trip here?" Brenda's mother asked.

"Not too bad," Kade's mother said. "That storm they were warning us about must have slipped past us."

"Good. We've had enough storms for this winter. I'm looking forward to spring again. You know, my garden catalog arrived the other day. I must have spent an hour just looking at the pictures."

Brenda, bored by the conversation, turned to Kade. "You look like a cute little caterpillar in that sleeping bag."

"Thanks, I've always wanted to be called a caterpillar."

A few minutes later Brenda's mother was called into the room to speak to President Mathesen. Kade's mother excused herself to go finish folding clothes.

"What's going on?" Brenda asked after they left.

"Beats me."

A few minutes later Emmet came in the room and sat down across from Kade and Brenda. "Brenda, something's come up that I need to talk to you about."

"I can leave if you want," Kade said.

"No, that's all right. Maybe you should hear it too." He paused. "President Mathesen has asked me to be a counselor in the branch presidency to help Kade's dad."

Brenda's mouth dropped open. "He asked *you*?"

"Yes."

"But you haven't even been going to church."

"I told him that. I told him everything, about drinking coffee and not paying tithing and swearing once in a while when I'm trying to fix something and hit my thumb with a hammer."

She grinned. "It's more than once in a while, Dad."

"I also told him about Kade's dad refusing us operating funds for next summer. It doesn't make sense for him and me to be working together in a church calling."

"What did he say?"

"He said he felt we could work it out."

"What are you going to do?"

"I told him I'd think about it and let him know in the morning. Let's go home now."

The clock struck one o'clock. Emmet sat alone at the kitchen table. He had gone to bed earlier, but after tossing and turning for more than an hour, he'd finally gotten up so he wouldn't keep Susan awake.

At one thirty Susan got up to see if he was all right.

"I've decided to say no," he said.

"I see."

"It doesn't make sense for me to work with Paul when he's trying to shut us down."

"Is that what he's trying to do?"

"Sure it is."

"Maybe he's really trying to help us."

"He's got a strange way of going about it then."

"Maybe he's right. Maybe we *are* too much in debt. It might not hurt to sell off some of our land."

"We'd take a big loss if we sold now."

"I know, but it'd cut way down on how much we owe."

"Whose side are you on anyway?"

"I haven't been able to sleep either. The question that keeps running through my mind is what if President Mathesen is right. What if this is a call from the Lord?"

"He probably says that to everyone."

"The point is he said it to you."

"It's too much to ask of a man to change his whole life-style overnight. I'd have to quit drinking coffee. I'd have to start going to church. I'd have to start paying tithing."

"Emmet, why haven't we been paying tithing?"

"We can't afford it."

"If you ask me, we can't afford not to."

"You think God will solve our problems if we start paying tithing?"

"No, I don't think that. But I'm pretty sure that paying tithing would help us more than it would hurt us. Emmet, we're in trouble. We could use a little help from God about now, couldn't we? How well have we managed on our own?"

"Someday I'll start paying tithing, but not now."

"Brenda's sixteen now. In a few years she's going to want to get married—in the temple, I hope. I want to be there with her, and I want you with me. Why don't we try doing things the Lord's way for a while and see if things work out any better?"

"You make everything sound so simple."

"Emmet, all our married life I've been waiting for you. Time is running out. My daughter needs a father who honors his priesthood so she'll want that in her home when she's married."

"There's other decent young men in the world besides Mormons. What about Doug? He comes from a good family, and he's got an interest in farming. He'd be a good husband for Brenda."

"You still don't know why she broke up with him, do you."

"No. Why did she?"

"Your precious Doug got drunk and tried to talk Brenda into going to bed with him."

"Did he do anything to her?"

"No, he just suggested it. That's all it took for Brenda. She made him take her home, and the next day she broke up with him."

"That sleazeball."

"That's why she spends so much time with Kade, because there's nobody else in school she trusts."

"Kade's a good boy."

"How can you say that and still not recognize how much the Church has helped to make him the way he is? I get so frustrated being your wife sometimes." She went back to bed.

Now Emmet felt worse than before.

At three o'clock Brenda got up to go to the bathroom. On her way back to bed, she saw him sitting in the kitchen. "Can't sleep, huh, Dad?"

"No."

She went over and began massaging his shoulders. "How's that?"

"Great. That'll probably put me right to sleep. Sit down, Brenda, and let's talk."

She sat down.

"Your mother says Doug tried to talk you into . . . " He cleared his throat. " . . . into going all the way with him."

Brenda blushed. "That's right. Nothing happened

though. Don't get mad at Doug. He was drunk at the time, so he probably didn't know what he was doing."

"That's no excuse."

"I know that."

"Why wasn't I told about it?"

"I don't know. I talked to Mom about it. I guess she didn't tell you because you always say what a great guy Doug is." She paused. "Also, I wasn't sure but what it might've been okay with you if I'd gone along with what Doug wanted."

"Why would you think that?"

"Because it might make it so I'd end up marrying him. That's what you want, isn't it, so that he and I can take over the farm someday? Besides, Mom is the one who talks about chastity. You never do."

"I feel the same way about it as your mother does."

"I guess I didn't know that for sure."

"Your mother says the reason you spend so much time with Kade is because he's the only boy in school you trust. Is that right?"

"Yes. Most of the guys in school my age drink a lot, so I end up with Kade. It's a little strange, him being only in the ninth grade and all. But he's a nice guy, and we're friends." She paused. "Of course, there's no big-time romance between us, but I guess he'll do until I go to BYU and meet—"she got a big grin on her face—"some real men."

"I feel like I don't even know you anymore. Where have I been all the time you've been growing up?"

"You've been busy."

He shook his head. "That's being too busy."

"Are you going to accept the calling, Dad?"

"I don't know. I've got six more hours to decide. You'd better go back to bed. Somebody in this family has to be awake enough tomorrow to drive."

When Susan got up at seven, she found Emmet in the kitchen, staring at a cup of coffee.

She sat down. "Are you going to drink that or what?"

"Coffee has such a wonderful smell, doesn't it? I mean, you will admit that, won't you?"

"Yes, it smells great."

"You walk into any office in town, and the first thing anyone asks is if you'd like a cup of coffee. And you say yes, and they give you a cup and sit around and talk, and it's like you're all good friends. It's great. Especially in the winter when it's forty below. A cup of coffee warms you up all the way down. No doubt about it, it's great to be a coffee drinker."

"Then why aren't you drinking it?"

He sighed. "I can't. Not anymore."

"Why not?"

"Do you know that Brenda thought that it might have been all right with me if she had gone to bed with Doug? She says I've never talked to her about morality. If it weren't for the things you taught her, she might've made a terrible mistake. Kade's done more to help her see what a man should be than I have. There's not much time left, but I've got to do what I can to be a good example for her." He paused. "I've decided to accept the calling in the branch presidency."

The next morning in sacrament meeting, President Mathesen was given time to conduct some business. "It is proposed that we sustain Emmet Sloan as first counselor in the branch presidency of the Shelby Branch. All those who can sustain Brother Sloan in this calling, please indicate by the uplifted hand." He looked over the congregation. "Any opposed? Thank you. It would be most appropriate now for Brother Sloan to come and take his place on the stand. We would like to hear a few words from him and then from his wife."

Emmet, a little uncomfortable in his suit, walked to the podium and nervously cleared his throat. "I was up all night trying to decide whether or not to accept this calling," he finally began. "I've had to do a lot of soul searching." He paused. "When a man looks back on his life and tries to decide what it all means, a lot of things you thought were important fall by the wayside. Sometimes you have to ask yourself, 'What's the most important thing in life?' All the things we own will be left behind when we die. But some things won't ever die. One is the love I have for my wife, Susan, and my daughter, Brenda. This church is important to the two people in my life I care the most about. So if it's important to them, maybe it should be important to me too. I need to learn more about the church. I need to find out how it can turn out a girl like Brenda and a boy like Kade. I don't know much about what exactly I'm supposed to do, but I promise you this—I'll do my very best." He sighed. "No matter what happens to my land."

After church, they gathered in the kitchen of the Odd Fellows hall, and there President Mathesen set apart Emmet.

On Tuesday night the two families got together for a potluck supper. Afterwards the two men went to Paul's office to talk and make plans. Kade and Brenda went into the living room to talk, while their mothers cleaned things up in the kitchen.

"Do you want to listen to some of the music my mom likes?" Kade asked.

"Sure, I guess so."

He put on a record of Beethoven's Fifth Symphony.

"You actually like this?" she asked.

"Yeah, sure, why not? I've been listening to it all my life. Even when I was little, my dad would take my sister and me to hear Mom play in the symphony. At first I had a hard time lasting all the way through it, but then my dad started giving me Lifesavers at the beginning of each concert. The thing I found out is that very few concerts last longer than one roll of Lifesavers. And after a while I actually started to enjoy it. I'll bet if you listened to classical music for a while, you'd learn to like it too."

"Maybe so." She paused. "You know what? You're a strange combination. Are you still lifting weights?"

"Yeah."

"I noticed your arms the other day. You're really turning into a hunk."

"I'm going to be taller and stronger than Jason before long."

"I bet you are too."

"Better looking too."

"Maybe so."

He gave up. "But not older."

"Right, not older."

"How are you and Jason getting along these days?" he asked.

"Good. His parents made him quit calling me because it was too expensive, so now we just write. We'll see each other next week at the youth dance."

"Do you miss him?"

"Yes, a lot. He's fun to be with. I like his sense of humor. He's always saying funny things."

"Like what?"

"Like when we were eating before the prom. He said the Chinese invented noodles and that spaghetti is a Chinese word meaning worms."

He looked at her. "That's not funny."

"Well, not now, but it was then."

"I could tell dumb jokes like that too."

"Kade, back off, okay? You're not in competition with him. I like him in a certain way and I like you in a different way." She paused. "I hate it when you get that puppy-dog look in your eyes."

"I want to go with someone," he said.

"You're not even sixteen. You're not supposed to date yet."

"I can think about it though, can't I?"

"I guess so."

"You've got Jason. Who've I got?"

"Linda."

"I want someone who lives around here."

"There's girls at school who like you."

"Who?"

"Lots of girls. Cynthia Rathlutner, for one."

"Cynthia Rathlutner?" He moaned. "You gotta be kidding."

"What's wrong with her? She's nice."

"Sure, if you like clarinet players."

"What's wrong with clarinet players?"

"Have you ever watched anyone play the clarinet? They sort of curl their bottom lip into their mouth, so it looks like they lost it in a fight with a bear."

"Kade, that's an awful thing to say."

"Then why are you laughing?"

"Because you're so funny sometimes."

"I'm funnier than Jason, that's for sure."

"There you go again."

"We do have good times together though, don't we?" he said.

"The best."

"I wish it could always be this way between us."

"It will be."

"What about when you go to college?"

"We'll still write to each other." She paused. "Besides, you won't always need me."

"How can you say that?"

"I can see it coming. You're like an eagle learning to fly. At first you go just a short distance and then come back to the nest, but one day you'll fly so high that you'll see how big and wonderful the world is, and you'll leave the nest and never come back."

He thought about it and then said, "That's the stupidest thing I've ever heard."

"It's not stupid, it's an analogy. When you get to be a junior, you'll learn about analogies."

"I don't care what it is, it's still dumb. I'm no eagle."

"What are you then?"

"A chipmunk."

"No, Kade, you're an eagle."

"In the first place, you're the one who's going to leave the stupid nest first. So if one of us is an eagle learning to fly, it's you, not me."

She paused. "Maybe we're both like young eagles learning to fly."

"Yeah, right," he scoffed. "You want something to eat? I thought I'd have ice cream, but, hey, since you're an eagle, maybe I can find you a live mouse."

"How dare you make fun of my analogies!" She chased after him, both of them giggling, through the kitchen and out the door.

The next weekend Paul and Emmet needed to go to Great Falls for a bishopric training session.

"How are you coming on getting an operating loan?" Paul asked as they rode along.

"Well, to tell you the truth, it's been a little disappointing. We haven't given up yet. It seems like if you're a poor risk with one bank, you're a poor risk with everybody."

"Maybe I can help. I could contact the places where you've applied and let them know that even though my hands are tied, I'm confident you're going to make it through this okay."

"You'd do that for me?"

"Of course."

"I don't want you to help me unless you do the same for the others." He paused. "How well do you know Harvey Mudlin?"

"Not very well."

"He's an awfully good man. If you just knew him better, I'm pretty sure you'd want to go to bat for him too. The same goes for the others. We can understand you might not be able to loan us any more money, but if you could at least show people you care about 'em, that'd lessen some of the resentment we feel at the way we've been treated lately."

On Monday morning Paul stood at the door of a farmhouse and knocked.

Harvey Mudlin came to the door. "What do you want?"

"I came to see how you were doing."

"How would you be doing if you were in my shoes?"

"Have you found another source for an operating loan yet?"

"Why are you asking? Have you changed your mind about helping us?"

"No."

"Then get off my property."

"Wait, hear me out first. I'd like to see what I can do to help out. I'm willing to put in a good word for you at wherever it is you've applied for a loan."

"Why would you do that?"

"Emmet Sloan and I were talking the other day. He thinks a lot of you. This morning I did some checking. You're one of the top producers in this area. It looks to me like if you go under, there's not much hope for anyone else. Harvey, this area needs you. I just want to do whatever I can to help."

"I guess you'd better come in then."

Two weeks later Paul got a phone call from Dwight Allen.

"Paul, how are things going out there on the frontier? You haven't frozen to death yet, have you?"

"Not yet."

"Good. Look, I just wanted to make sure you've refused operating loans to the four we talked about."

"Yes."

"They can't farm without operating loans. Have any of them decided to sell out?"

"No. They got operating loans from other sources."

Dwight was surprised. "All of them?"

"Yes."

"How did they manage to do that?"

"I helped them."

"You what?"

"I went and talked to the loan officers at the places they applied to for loans."

"Your mind is turning to mush, Paul."

"That's not it."

"How do you explain it then?"

"It doesn't have anything to do with the mind, Dwight. It has to do with the heart."

With Paul Ellis's help, Emmet and the others were able to obtain operating loans for the summer. And so with another season assured, the pressure eased up some. Now all the four farmers had to worry about was if they'd have rain but not hail and if the price of wheat would be high enough so they could make a decent living—or at least break even.

At the end of April Paul and Emmet went to Great Falls for a stake leadership meeting. Kade and Brenda rode along because a home-study seminary Super Saturday lesson and activity were scheduled at the same time. Paul drove, with Emmet in the front seat and Brenda and Kade in the back.

Because she treated Kade like one of the family, Brenda slept for an hour, then woke up and brushed her hair and put on makeup.

"Going all out, are we?" Emmet kidded her. "Poor Jason doesn't stand a chance."

She smiled. "I hope not."

Kade figured Jason would be waiting for Brenda in the foyer of the church when they arrived, but he wasn't. Kade and Brenda walked to the seminary room together. Brenda looked for Jason. He saw her but didn't get up from where he was sitting, which was next to a girl with long blond hair.

"It's time to start now. Everyone take a seat," the teacher in charge announced.

Kade and Brenda found two empty seats and sat down. They had a good view of Jason. He was talking to the other girl.

After an opening song and a prayer and some announcements, the lesson began. Brenda kept her eyes on Jason and the blond girl. She leaned forward and asked the girl in front of her, "What's the name of that girl with Jason?"

"That's Amy. She's going with him."

Brenda's face turned a bright red. "Excuse me," she said. She got up and left the room.

Kade waited for her to come back, but she didn't, so he left to go find her. He walked through the building and went outside. She was standing by the car in the parking lot. He went over and stood beside her.

"I'm sorry," he said.

She nodded. Her eyes were moist but she wasn't crying.

"Are you going to talk to him?" Kade asked.

"No."

"You should. You should tell him what a puke-face he is. That's what I'd do."

"You're not me."

"You can't just let him get away with this. The least he could've done was to phone and tell you he didn't want to go with you anymore."

"We weren't going together."

"I know, but he kissed you. He shouldn't have kissed you unless he wanted to go with you."

"Maybe if I lived here, things would've been different. We only saw each other once a month."

"Why are you taking his side? The guy's a creep, that's all there is to it." He pulled out a set of car keys from his pocket. "You want to go for a ride?"

"Your dad doesn't want you driving around when you're supposed to be in a meeting."

"He'll never know. We can go anywhere you want. Just say the word. You want to go to the mall?"

"No. Let's go back inside."

"But Jason is there with Amy."

"I don't care. Let's go in." She started to walk away.

"Wait a minute."

"What?"

"Let me take over where Jason left off."

She frowned. "It can't ever be like that for us."

"Why not?"

"It just can't."

"I love you."

She closed her eyes as if it were bad news. "I know that."

"I'm taller than you now, and I have a driver's license."

"Kade, will you stop it? I've told you a hundred times how I feel. Why can't you just accept it and quit bothering me all the time?"

She went back inside.

He stewed for a while and then went back to the meeting, but he didn't sit next to her.

On the way home after the meeting, Brenda started reading a paperback novel. Kade, still hurt by her rejection, curled up and eventually went to sleep.

When he woke up, he glanced over at Brenda. She was asleep, the book on her lap. He closed his eyes and tried to go back to sleep, but it was no use.

His dad and Emmet were talking. "You want to know

something?" Emmet said. "I like being in the branch presidency."

"Good. I like having you there."

"If you want to know the truth, I'm a little surprised I can do the job."

"Why?"

"You know what they say, 'You can't teach an old dog new tricks.' "

"You're not exactly old."

"I know, but it's so easy to get in a rut. In leadership meeting today, when they started asking questions, I surprised myself because I knew the answers. It's like I'm discovering a part of me I never knew existed." He paused. "You know when they had us split up into small groups? Well, we got done before the other groups, so I started talking to the bishop of one of the wards in Great Falls. He's in the motel business. You might know him—Dennis McKinnon?"

"Sure, I've met him."

"He got to talking about his job, and all of a sudden I realized he gets paid every week. He pretty much knows how much money he's going to make this year. I thought to myself, isn't that amazing? I bet when he goes home at night, he can devote his energies to his family. I thought how lucky he is not to have a cloud hanging over his head twenty-four hours a day like I do."

"Even that isn't one hundred percent certain. If people quit staying at his motel, he'll lose money."

"Oh sure, but let's say that he does some things so his motel is full every night. He makes more money, right?"

"That's the way it works, all right."

"In farming, if you have a bumper crop, the price drops and you lose income." He paused. "Today I realized how much pressure is on me these days."

"You ready to be a motel manager?" Paul asked.

"No, but you know what? I could be if I wanted to."
He sighed. "Of course, my dad would probably never speak to me again if I sold the place and pulled up stakes. He thinks the land has to remain in the family. I used to think that too, but now I'm not so sure. I guess I'm getting tired of all the time saying, 'Next year will be better.' It never is. Besides, who cares about farmers? Nobody."

"The reports that come across my desk predict a bumper grain crop this year," Paul said.

"I hope so. Not just for me, but for everybody. We're hurting these days. We really need a good year."

"Is Kade asleep?" Paul asked.

Emmet turned back. "Yeah. Why?"

"I was wondering if you could give me some advice."

"Advice about Kade? You don't need advice. You and Denise are doing a great job."

"Maybe so, but I've seen the way he lights up when he's around you. You're his favorite adult right now. I was just wondering what your secret is."

"Look, the only thing I've done is to put him to work when he comes around."

"You've done more for him than that. That set of barbells you made was the best Christmas gift he ever received."

"I'm glad to be Kade's friend, but one thing I'm sure of. When he gets older, he's going to see what a great man you are. When that happens, a set of homemade barbells isn't going to amount to a hill of beans."

"I just want to be what Kade needs me to be."

Kade felt the tears coming. Still pretending to be asleep, he turned so nobody could see.

"Emmet, you think that maybe someday you and I and Kade and Brenda could do something together?"

"You want to go camping?"

"Sure, why not?"

"All right. We'll do that real soon."

Kade heard Brenda moving, waking up from her nap. "How much longer?" she asked.

"Two thousand miles. We've decided to go to California," Emmet said.

"Oh, sure. President Ellis, I know you'll tell me the truth. How close are we to Shelby?"

"We'll be there in half an hour."

"And then we're going to California," Emmet added.

On Monday students signed up for the classes they wanted to take in the fall. On the way home after school, Kade asked Brenda if she'd signed up for art.

She paused. "No, I forgot."

"You said you'd take it with me."

She sighed. "I know, but I already have a full schedule."

"But you promised."

"Look, you have to learn to stand on your own two feet. You're the artist, not me. If you want to take an art class, then go ahead, but leave me out of it."

"But you promised."

"Why is it so important I take art with you?"

"I just want to have a class with you."

"Why? So you can pretend you're the same age as me?"

That hurt. "Just forget the whole stupid thing then."

"Are you going to take the class?" she asked.

"No."

"Why not."

"It wouldn't be the same."

"What are you trying to do, punish me? Sometimes you make me so mad. If you acted more grown up, then maybe we'd get along better. The kind of guy who interests me is someone who can stand on his own two feet. Don't go around trying to please me all the time. Decide what you want out of life and then go for it.

After I leave for college, you won't have me around to tell you what to do every step of the way."

When Kade got home, he went to his room to work out. He took off his shirt, picked up the barbell, and did an arm curl. He looked at his reflection in the mirror. He was a lot stronger than he used to be, but he wondered if it made any difference to Brenda. All this time he'd been trying to impress her one way when what she really wanted from him was something else. The only trouble was, he wasn't quite sure what she wanted.

After supper he asked his father if they could take a walk together. "Sure, let me change my shoes first, okay?"

They walked out past the barn. "Dad, I need some advice. I've got this summer and one more year of school before Brenda goes away to college. Before she leaves, I want her to like me the same way I like her. At first I thought it'd happen when I got to be stronger. That's partly why I've been working out. But today she told me some things that made me realize I don't understand her very well."

"What did she say?"

"She wants me not to depend on her so much. Does that make sense?"

"It might. Brenda has a very strong personality. She probably looks for that in others."

"Do you think I'll ever stand a chance with her?"

"I don't know, Kade. She *is* two years older than you. One thing in your favor, though—she chooses to spend time with you over any other guy in school. That must mean something."

"Sure. It means I'm the only guy in school who doesn't drink."

"Is that really true?"

"I don't know. It seems like it."

"I'm glad you haven't gone along with the crowd. I know it must not be easy at times."

"It's all right because of Brenda."

"You're both lucky to have each other. No matter what happens, you'll always be good friends."

"That's not enough." He paused. "I'll try being more independent and see how that works."

At school the next day, Kade set about proving that he could set his own course. First he approached the art teacher. "Mrs. Felton, can I talk to you for a minute?"

"Yes, what is it?"

He pulled out the drawing he'd done of Brenda and him in the barn after the prom. "I drew this."

She looked at it. "It's very good."

"I'm going to take art next year. I just wanted you to know."

"Is that all?" she asked.

"Yes, why?"

"Most people who bring me something ask if they have any talent. You didn't do that. Why not?"

"I already know I have talent."

She smiled. "You'll do fine. I'll look forward to having you in class."

An hour later, as Coach Brannigan ended another boys' gym, Kade approached him in the gym. "Can I talk to you?"

"Sure, Kade, what's up?"

"I've decided to go out for football next fall."

"What position?"

"A kicker."

"We don't have a separate kicker on our team."

"You will next year."

"What makes you think you can kick a football?"

"I played soccer in Illinois."

"Soccer isn't football."

"I'm going to practice all summer. I'm going to help the team win some games next fall, Coach. You'll see."

Kade could tell the coach wasn't convinced. He went to the rope hanging from the ceiling, lifted himself hand over hand to the top, and then lowered himself back down. "Coach, I don't suppose you could change my grade to an A now, could you?"

"What's got into you?"

"I'm just growing up, that's all. Look, I need a favor from you this summer."

"What?"

"I need to borrow some practice footballs. I'll need a supply so I can practice kicking without chasing after one ball all the time."

"I don't loan out school property over the summer."

"Coach, how much did we lose that last game by?"

"By a field goal."

"That's why you need a kicker. Give me a chance to show you what I can do."

The coach thought about it. "All right, come see me the last week of school, and I'll check out some footballs to you."

On the way home from school that day, Kade told Brenda what he'd done. "So, what do you think?" he asked.

She scowled. "I think you just ruined it."

"How?"

"By asking me what I thought. It's like you did it all just to impress me. If you want to play football, then play football, but don't do it just to impress me. It's your life, not mine."

"What do you want from me anyway? You're impossible to talk with anymore."

"Maybe we shouldn't see so much of each other for a while."

"Fine, no problem. I don't need you."

They drove in silence for several miles. "I'd still like to pick you up in the morning though," she finally said.

"Why?"

"Because your dad is helping with the gas and, well, the truth is we need the money, so let me keep picking you up. Okay?"

"There's only three more weeks of school. I guess I can stand it till then."

The next morning when he got in her pickup to ride to seminary, he brought with him a portable tape deck. He turned it on until it was louder than the music coming from her radio.

"What are you doing?" she yelled above the noise.

"Today we're going to listen to what I want."

"It's too noisy in here. Turn it off."

"No. You turn your radio off. You're getting paid to drive me into town, so be a good cab driver and do what I say."

She could see he wasn't going to back down, so she turned off her radio. "Honestly, Kade."

"What?"

"Why don't you grow up?"

"That's what I'm doing. Hey, if you cooperate, maybe I'll have my dad put in a couple of dollars extra at the end of the month. That's all you've cared about all this time anyway, isn't it?"

"You're hopeless."

"Good. That's what I want to be."

They listened to "Night on Bald Mountain." It sounded the way Kade felt — dangerous and a little out of control.

In school he saw Whitney Lundquist in the library. "Mind if I sit down?" he asked.

"No."

"What are you doing?"

"I have to read a book," she said.

"I hate it when that happens," he joked. "So, how are things going for you?"

"Can't complain."

"You want to go out with me sometime?" he asked.

"I'm going with Doug."

"You're kidding."

"No. What's wrong with Doug?"

"Nothing. It's just that I knew a girl who used to go with him, that's all."

"You mean Brenda Sloan?"

"Yeah."

"Doug's told me about her. The way Doug tells it, she should be a nun."

"Do you and Doug get along okay?"

"Yeah, fine. Why?"

"Just wondering. Is he still drinking?"

"Of course. We both are. What else is there to do around here?"

"Not much." He stood up. "Just be careful on the roads, okay?"

She smiled. "You sound like my mom."

He started to leave and then paused. "Brenda and I are Mormons."

"So?"

"I just wanted you to know."

"Why?"

"If things ever get bad for you, promise me you'll look into the Mormon church."

"Things are never going to get bad for me, Kade. I got things figured out."

"I know, but if they ever do."

She looked at him strangely. "You believe in your church, Kade?"

"Yeah, I do."

"And yet you know I like to party and have fun, right? So if you're such a great Mormon, why did you just ask me out?"

"Good question."

"I thought so too."

"I guess I was trying to get back at somebody."

"Who?"

"Brenda."

"Why?"

"I want to go with her."

"She's too old for you."

"Look who's talking. Doug's older than you."

"That's different."

"Why is it different?"

"It just is."

"Brenda's the only girl I'm interested in. I want to go with her, but she just wants me for a friend."

When he met Brenda in the parking lot after school, he said, "I need to talk to you."

"What about?"

"I'm sorry for the way I acted this morning."

"No problem. I figured you'd snap out of it eventually."

"I don't know what happened. Things got really crazy there for a while."

"Things are changing between us, Kade. That's what's making all the fireworks. I'm beginning to think of you as more of, well, an equal. When you don't act the way I think you should, it makes me mad. The fact is, I've been really getting mad at you lately. Sorry."

"I guess a friendship is a growing thing," he said.

"Yeah, I guess so."

On the last day of school, instead of going straight home, they stopped at a grocery store and bought some food and then drove to a lake and had a picnic. They talked about going swimming, but there was a brisk northerly wind and the water was too cold. He was wearing a cowboy hat because when he got up that morning he felt wild and crazy—crazy enough to wear what the locals wore every day.

They sat at a picnic table overlooking the lake. "Another year bites the dust," Brenda said, pulling off a clump of grapes from the bunch they'd brought.

"Yeah, right."

"One more year for me and then I'm off to BYU."

"BYU has too many students," he said.

She smiled. "That's why I'm going there. I want to be someplace that's crawling with Mormons."

"You mean crawling with Mormon guys."

"What's so bad about that?"

"Nothing. I know you need that."

"You make it sound like a weakness. What's wrong with me liking guys?"

"Nothing."

"Wait till you get back from your mission. You'll be singing a different tune then. I'd love to be around to watch you trying to catch up after two years of not dating."

"I won't be like that."

"You will so. You'll have five or six dates every weekend. I want to be in the background, laughing at the way you'll be carrying on."

"By that time you'll be married and have two or three kids."

"Not me. I'm in no hurry to get married. I'm just going to play the field."

"No way. You'll marry the first guy you find at BYU that looks halfway decent."

"Not me."

"You will. You even drool over the missionaries."

"That's not true."

"Don't give me that. I've seen you talking to them after church."

"You're supposed to talk to people after church, so they'll feel welcome," she said.

"Oh, they feel welcome around you. Yes sir, no problem there."

"You're not going to rile me this time, so just drop it, okay? You want another sandwich?"

"I suppose."

"Did my dad talk to you yet?" she asked.

"What about?"

"He's going to ask you if you want to work around our place this summer."

"For money?"

"Of course for money. What do you think?"

"I don't know much about farming."

"Much? Let's face it, you don't know beans about farming. It doesn't matter. Dad and I'll teach you all you need to know. What do you say?"

"You wouldn't be my boss, would you?" he asked.

"Why, couldn't you handle that?"

"You're not an easy person to get along with, in case you didn't know."

"Hey, just do what I say and there won't be any problem. When I say jump, you say, 'How high?' Got the picture?"

"I'd rather pick up pop cans along the highway than be under your thumb."

"Just kidding. Actually, my dad'll be the boss."

"That'd be okay."

"It looks like it's going to be good year for us. The winter wheat is looking good. We had plenty of snow this winter so the sub-soil moisture is looking real good."

He smiled.

"What's so funny?" she asked.

"It's so weird to hear you talk like a farmer."

"You ought to hear my Grampa." Her expression grew serious. "He and Gramma are coming back for a visit next week. I hope we can stand it."

"Why do you say that?"

"It's what Grampa does to my dad that I don't like."

"What do you mean?"

"Dad took over the place when Grampa retired, but

the way Grampa talks, it's still his place, and we're just working it for him. He finds fault with every little thing my dad's changed since he left. A lot of the time he treats my dad like he was still a kid."

"That must be tough to take. Life's kind of rough sometimes, isn't it? Even when you're grown up."

"Yeah, it doesn't seem to get any easier," she said. "What do you want to be when you grow up?"

"A football coach. Coach Biff Ellis of the Chicago Bears. It has a nice ring to it, doesn't it?"

She unceremoniously pulled his hat over his head. He chased her but she was too fast for him, so he went back to the table.

A minute later she came up behind him and leaned on his shoulders. "Hey, coach, you ready for dessert now?"

"Sure, why not?"

She got a package of donuts and a carton of milk from the paper sack. "We forgot to get glasses."

"We can trade off drinking from the carton."

"We'll get each other's germs that way."

"I can take it, I've got my cowboy hat on."

"Since it was my fault, you can take the first swig of milk."

While they ate, they watched white puffy clouds race toward them from Canada.

"You know what?" she said. "There's nobody I enjoy talking to more than you."

"It wasn't that way in the beginning."

"Gosh no. You were a real pain when I first started picking you up. There you were, Mr. Goody Two Shoes, with your little angel face, all eager and ready for school. You seemed like such a little kid. I could hardly stand you at first."

"And now look at us," he said, "sharing a carton of milk together and grossing out on donuts."

"No doubt about it, we've come a long ways."

"Just one more year of school and then you'll go off to college."

"That's right."

"That'll be tough to take, for me anyway."

"For me too. But hey, it's over a year away. No use talking about it now." She looked at the setting sun. "I think it's time to go."

On their way back they had several miles to go on a dirt road before they got to the highway. She gunned the pickup so they'd have a wild ride.

"Slow down, okay?" he called out.

"What's the matter, cowboy? Can't you take it?"

"I mean it. Slow down before you kill us both."

She slowed down. A minute later she turned on the radio. He sang along, adding a cowboy twang in his voice.

They sang all the way home.

A week after Kade started working at the farm Brenda's grandparents arrived. In the afternoon on the third day of their visit, Brenda, Kade, and Emmet were out near the barn trying to fix the tractor when Brenda's grandfather stormed out of the house and over to them. "Susan just told me you're thinking about selling some land."

"That's right. If I can find a buyer," Emmet said.

"You can't be serious."

"I don't have much choice. The bank says I'm way too much in debt."

"What's got into you? You can't sell land that's been in the family for five generations."

"Dad, with due respect, you don't have any say in this. I'm the one who makes the decisions around here now."

"I thought I could trust you to carry on the family heritage."

"It's fine and good to talk about family heritage when times are good, but the truth is we end up losing money every year. I'm not sure how much longer I can keep it up, even for the sake of family heritage. There's other ways to make a living, you know."

"This is a whole lot more than just making a living."

"Dad, it's not that anymore."

"I was able to do okay here. Why can't you?"

"Things are different now."

"Not that different. If that's the way you feel, why don't you just sell off the farm and get a job in some factory?"

"Maybe I will," Emmet said.

"You can't be serious."

"I'm thinking about it. I guess it depends on how well we do this summer. This place is eating us alive. All we do is worry about making payments and whether or not we'll get a loan to get us through the next season. If what you're doing to make a living doesn't pay you to do it, maybe it's time for a change. There's more important things in life than holding onto a parcel of land."

"Like what?"

"Like my family."

"There's no better way to raise a family than on a farm."

"Maybe that was true a few years ago, but I'm not sure it is now."

"I can't believe I'm hearing this from you. I never pegged you as a quitter."

"I've got to live my life the way that's best for me. Maybe I'll stay and maybe I won't, I just don't know. A lot depends on how well we do this summer."

"Brenda, what about you? Do you have any interest in carrying on here after your dad retires?"

"I don't know. Dad and I work so hard and yet we're just barely getting by. I'm not sure I want that."

"In my day people had loyalty to their land." Emmet's father, his face red and his jaws clamped shut, turned and stormed back to the house to talk to his wife.

Brenda's grandparents left as soon as they could get packed. Emmet tried to talk them into staying the night, but his dad, still fuming, said he thought it'd be best if they got a good start before nightfall.

"Well, at least that's over," Emmet said as his parents drove away.

Brenda and Kade didn't always get along as they worked.

"Let me show you," Brenda said when Kade tried to tighten the wire as they mended fence.

"I know what I'm doing."

"I know, but just let me show you."

"I don't want your help."

"Kade, let me do it. You're messing it up."

"No I'm not."

"I'm telling you—you're doing it all wrong."

"All right then, you do it."

"Now watch me. And don't be so pig-headed next time. All right?"

"You're not strong enough to do that. That's man's work."

"You don't have to be strong, you just have to be smart. That's why I can do it and you can't." She finished. "There, how's that?" She popped the hammer on the wire. It was so tight it sang.

"Not bad," he grudgingly admitted.

"Not bad? Face it, Kade, it's perfect. You saw how I did it. You do it that way from now on. You agree my way is better, don't you?"

"Not that much better."

"It's so hard for you to admit a girl is better at some things, isn't it."

"You have an unfair advantage."

"What's that?"

"Your dad raised you like a son."

"He raised me to work, that's all. I'm better than you at this, and I always will be. You better get used to it. You're going to run into it the rest of your life."

"I'm still better at drawing than you."

"That's for sure. Are you still drawing?"

"Yeah, when I'm not too tired."

"Pictures of me?"

"You're so conceited. You think all I do is daydream about you?"

"Who else have you drawn lately?"

"I did one of your dad. It's a closeup of his face after a long day."

"Have you ever done a picture of your dad?"

"No."

"Why not?"

"I don't know."

"You think you might take him for granted sometimes?"

"Maybe."

"You've got a wonderful dad, Kade."

"I suppose."

"You think you'll turn out to be like him?"

"Probably not."

"I think you will." She paused. "At least I hope you do." She looked out over the fields, then back at Kade. "It's been fun watching you grow up. Your voice has dropped about an octave just lately. And you're getting so tall. I really think you're going to turn out okay. Don't forget I had a part in it. Be sure and tell the girl you marry how much I did to help you turn out halfway decent."

At night after work they sometimes drove to town and cruised Main Street like everybody else their age, but usually after a couple of passes they got bored and did something else. A couple of times a week they went swimming at the city pool. During the day it was full of little kids and mothers, but in the evening, the crowd thinned out and high school youth and college students home for the summer took over.

When Kade and Brenda were together, either lying

down by the side of the pool or bobbing in the water next to each other, other guys would mostly leave her alone, but Brenda knew how to dive and Kade didn't, so sometimes she was practicing diving while he was lying down on the still-warm cement.

One time when they were separated, a college student, working in town for the summer, asked if she wanted to go with him to a party.

"I guess not. Thanks anyway."

"Why not?"

"I already have a date."

"Who?"

"That guy over there."

"Oh. How come he leaves you alone so much of the time."

"He doesn't dive."

"He should pay more attention to you, or he'll lose you."

She smiled. "I'll tell him. Thanks."

Sometimes after swimming, they'd drive over to the high school football field. They'd drive her pickup out onto the cinder track and she'd keep the motor running with the headlights on so they could see in the dark. Then she'd hold the ball for him while he practiced kicking extra points and field goals. After a few weeks Kade got so he could make it from the twenty-yard line about half the time.

"You're getting better, Kade."

"Yeah, too bad you can't hold the ball for me in the games."

"I'd like to do that. You want to ask Coach Brannigan?"

"Not really. He'd say that football is no game for a girl."

"But we know different, don't we," she said with a grin.

One night while they were practicing, another car

drove up and stopped. Two people got out, but Kade couldn't see who they were because they were still behind the light from the headlights.

"Well, look here," a voice said. "It's Kade Ellis, the boy wonder." Doug stepped out into the light. He had Whitney with him. "What are you doing this time of night?"

"Practicing kicking field goals," Kade said. "I'm going out for the football team in the fall."

"You think you're man enough for that?"

"Sure, no problem."

Doug spotted Brenda. "Well, I see you're still chasing little boys."

"Kade's not so little anymore though, is he," she said.

"Hi, Brenda," Whitney said. "How's it going?"

"Can't complain. How about you?"

"Okay. Did you know Doug and I are getting married?" Whitney asked.

"No, I didn't know that. When?"

"As soon as possible," Whitney said.

"Will you still be going to Montana State to play football?" Kade asked Doug.

"No. The football scholarship didn't come through like I thought it would. So I'll be staying here and helping my dad."

"Sounds great."

"It's not."

Kade hesitated and then said, "You don't sound too happy about it."

"Haven't you heard?" Doug said. "Whitney's gone and got herself pregnant."

"You don't have to go around announcing it to the whole world, do you?" Whitney complained.

"People around here can count to nine, so why not just come out and admit it?"

"I'd just like to be treated with a little respect, that's all."

"Seems to me it's a little late for respect."

"Is this how you're going to treat me from now on?"

"If it weren't for you, I'd be going to college in the fall." He turned to Kade. "She refused to get it fixed."

"By getting it fixed, he means getting an abortion," Whitney said.

"You did the right thing," Brenda said to Whitney.

"You women always stick together, don't you," Doug said, sneering.

"Abortions are wrong," Brenda said.

There was an uncomfortable silence. "Well, let's go, Gus," Doug said.

"Don't call me that," Whitney said.

"You're so hard to get along with these days."

Brenda watched them drive away. "That's so sad. Poor Whitney."

They drove home listening to the music on the radio. Just before pulling up to let him out, she said, "Kade, thanks for being my friend."

"Yeah, sure."

She stopped in front of his house. They sat there in the dark. She reached over and tossled his hair. Somehow she seemed different. "You know what?" she asked softly.

"What?"

"You're getting to be one handsome dude."

He wondered if that meant she'd let him kiss her if he tried. Frantically he tried to figure out what to do. Finally he worked out a plan. He would scoot over next to her and then yawn and stretch. With his arms still outstretched, he'd casually put his arm around her shoulder and then lean over and kiss her.

He scooted as close as he could get, but the gearshift knob was in his way. Even so, he was still within arm's length. He yawned and stretched according to plan.

"Are you tired?" she asked.

It was a difficult question to answer. "Yeah, I guess so."

"I'd better go then so you can get some sleep. We've got a full day tomorrow. See you in the morning."

"Yeah, right." Bewildered, he got out and watched her drive away.

That night he had a hard time sleeping because he kept playing the scene over and over in his mind, trying to decide where he'd gone wrong.

One thing he decided—yawning was definitely not the way to go.

Emmet sat in his pickup on top of a knoll looking out at his land, now ripe with wheat, ready to be harvested.

"You're going to have a good year," Darrell Brekhus, a representative for an agri-business firm, said.

"Looks that way, if it doesn't hail before the combine crews get here."

"I like what you've shown me. Of course, I'll have to make a few phone calls to make it official, but I'm fairly certain we'll take it."

"Great."

"Actually, if you want to know the truth, we'd rather just buy the whole farm."

"Are you serious?"

"Absolutely. We could make you a pretty good offer on the place."

"It'd be tough to just walk away. This place has been in the family a long time."

"When's the last time you had a good crop like this?"

"Three years ago."

"It's hard to make money when you lose money two out of every three tries."

"You're not telling me anything I don't already know."

"Think about it, Emmet. I'll be in town at the Tip Top Motel until tomorrow at noon."

That night Emmet phoned his father.

"Is everyone all right?" his father asked, believing that you don't phone long distance unless there's a death in the family.

"Everyone's fine." Emmet cleared his throat. "Dad, I have an opportunity to sell the place. Susan and I've talked it over. We think it might be for the best. At least we'd leave the place with a little nest egg. That's better than the ones who've ended up losing everything."

"What on earth would you do for a living?"

"I have a friend in Great Falls. He's a member of the Church. He runs a motel. I called him this afternoon to ask his opinion. He told me he's building a ski lodge in Vail, Colorado. He asked me if I'd like to manage it."

"You don't know anything about managing a motel."

"I can learn."

"Sounds like you've already made your decision."

"I guess maybe we have."

"Then why did you call me?"

"To get your blessing."

"You want me to tell you it's all right to give up? You want me to tell you it's all right to sell off a farm that's been in the family for all these years? Well, forget it. I know what you're after. You want me to ease your conscience just because you don't have the gumption to last out a few bad years. Well, forget it. You do what you want, but don't come crying to me when you're out of a job and wish you still had the farm to fall back on." With that, his father hung up.

Emmet slowly put the phone back. "He hung up on me," he told Susan.

She touched his shoulder. "I know this is hard for

him, but he's got to understand we have to live our lives the way we think is best for us."

"Do you think we're doing the right thing?" he asked.

"I don't know. What do you think?"

"It's been a long time since farming was any fun for me."

"Then maybe it's time to move on. Will you miss it?"

"Yes, very much."

"Me too."

"It ought to be possible to make a living farming here, but for some reason it doesn't seem like it is anymore."

She came to him, and he held her in his arms for a long time. Then he sighed, pulled away, and said softly, "We'd better go tell Brenda."

Vehicles were parked all over the yard with the overflow lined up alongside the road. The auctioneer's voice boomed over the PA system. Kade and Brenda stood on the edge of the crowd and watched until it got too painful for her. Then she asked him to take her for a drive.

He was driving his dad's car. He pulled out onto the road and turned the radio to the country-western station she liked. They left a trail of dust behind them as they sped along the gravel road. She looked out her window but didn't say anything.

"Where do you want to go?"

"To town, I guess."

When they got to town, she had him drive past the school once and then down Main Street slowly.

"Do you want to stop anywhere?" he asked.

"No."

He turned onto Interstate 15, heading north in the direction of Canada. He imagined they were running away to start a new life. They'd find an apartment in Calgary and nobody would know where they were. He wanted the dream to stay but reality kept seeping through. He knew it could never be.

"You're kind of quiet," she said.

"Yeah."

"What are you thinking about?"

"Nothing."

"I'm going to miss you, Kade."

"Yeah, sure." He clipped the words short.

"Are you mad at me for leaving?"

"No."

"Kade, this is our last time together."

"So?"

"Tell me what you're thinking."

"That I'll never let myself be hurt like this again."

"I'm hurting too."

"Not like me. You never needed me as much as I needed you."

"That's not true, Kade."

"Yes it is."

"What am I ever going to do with you?" she said.

"Nothing, because it's over."

"It'll never be over. Even though we won't see each other very much from now on, we'll always be in each other's thoughts. We helped each other grow up. You can't just cut me out of your thoughts, because if you do, you'll end up losing a part of yourself."

"I have lost a part of myself, the best part. I've lost you."

Suddenly it was too much for him to hold in, and tears started to come. He was ashamed of having her see him this way, but he couldn't seem to stop. It wasn't safe for him to drive anymore; he pulled over onto the side of the road.

She came to his side, and they threw their arms around each other and cried.

Brenda was right—he never forgot her. She was in his thoughts during the first football game of the season when after two misses he finally kicked his first field goal. He thought of her the first day he walked into art class. When the teacher asked the class why they were taking the course, he said, "I have a friend who saw some drawings I'd done. She told me I should take this class. Actually we were going to take it together."

"Who was it?" someone asked.

"Brenda Sloan. She moved to Colorado."

"She's older than you, isn't she?" a girl next to him asked.

"Yeah, but we were friends anyway."

For weeks after Brenda left, he drew nothing but the barren windswept fields of November; that was how he felt. But then one day he drew a picture of an old Indian man with a weather-beaten face. He had seen the man one day in the hardware store. The next day he drew a picture of the football team practicing on a clear, crisp October afternoon. That opened the floodgate of drawings again.

"Life goes on" is something you hear in small towns from people who have seen their share of disappointment and heartache. Kade heard it often growing up in western Montana. Strangely enough, though, he found it to be true. Life did go on without Brenda.

His family stayed in Shelby through his high school years, even though his father was asked to move to the corporate headquarters in Chicago. Paul turned down what would have been a promotion because he was the branch president and didn't want to leave until he accomplished getting a building finished, and also because he didn't want to move until Kade graduated from high school.

Kade became an important addition to the football team. In his senior year during the final game of the state football championship tournament, he kicked three field goals and two extra-point conversions. Shelby won, 23 to 21. Kade was one of the players the coach singled out for praise when he was interviewed by the Shelby radio station after the game.

During his senior year of high school, Kade and Linda Cooper became close friends. She was the first girl he ever kissed. He wrote to her often his senior year, and went to Great Falls every chance he got to be with her.

After he graduated from high school, he worked at the bank until it was time for his mission. By this time Brenda was at BYU. They wrote once in a while just to let the other know how things were going.

Kade served a mission in Guatemala. While there, his father was promoted to the bank's corporate offices in Chicago, so when Kade returned home from his mission, he didn't go back to Montana.

The day after he arrived home from his mission, he phoned Emmet in Colorado and asked about Brenda. He hadn't heard anything from her for a long time.

"She's at BYU still," Emmet said. "This is her junior year. She dropped out for a while to come help us out at the ski lodge." He paused. "I had an operation and it kind of slowed me down for a while, so we needed her to help us out."

"How are you doing now?" Kade asked.

"As mean and ornery as ever. When are you going to come and visit us?"

"One of these days."

A week later Kade left to start fall semester at Ricks College in Rexburg, Idaho, majoring in business management. He had chosen Ricks because Linda Cooper was there. After their first date, though, she told him she'd found someone else and that he'd asked her to marry him.

"What did you tell him?" Kade asked.

"I told him I had to wait until you got home."

"I'm not ready to get married," he said.

They broke up shortly after that.

During Christmas vacation at his family's new home near Chicago, Kade found the Monopoly box containing the sketches of Brenda. Each one brought back rich memories.

The next semester, just for fun, he decided to take "Introduction to Oil Painting." He enjoyed the course immensely. He'd forgotten how fulfilling art was. He often stayed up late at night and worked. He began to use his earlier drawings of Brenda as a starting place for his paintings.

One day the art instructor suggested that he major in art, but Kade told him he had decided to major in business.

"Why business?"

"Because you can help people if you're in business."

"I've never heard that before."

"That's because you don't know my dad."

"Who's the girl in all your paintings?"

"Just a girl I used to know. Her name is Brenda."

"In this one, she's wearing a formal in an old barn, dancing with a boy who's obviously younger than her. Is that supposed to be symbolic?"

"Not really. It happened just the way I've drawn it. It was after the junior prom."

"Did you take her to the prom?"

"No, I was too young. She came by and woke me up and asked me to come have the last dance with her."

"Why did she do that?"

"It's a long story."

"I think you should enter that painting in a contest BYU is sponsoring."

"What for?"

"More people than just you should see it. How about it?"

"I don't think so, but thanks for suggesting it anyway."

"Would you object if I entered it under your name?"

"It won't win."

"Just let me enter it."

"All right."

The instructor studied the painting. "Were you in love with her?"

"I don't know how to explain the way it was between us. If I said we were in love, you wouldn't understand the way it really was. The closest I can come to what it was like is to say we were best friends."

The painting entitled "Brenda at the Prom" took second place in the contest. Kade was invited to BYU to exhibit his painting and to meet with some of the faculty of the Art Department.

On the opening night of the exhibit, he was asked to stand beside his painting to talk to anyone who might have questions.

A professor came up and looked closely at the painting. "I like this very much. Are you going to major in art?"

"Probably not."

"Why not?"

Kade smiled. "I want a steady income."

"You could have one if you'd keep painting."

A minute later Kade turned around and saw Brenda standing there. It almost took his breath away to see her again. "Hello," he said, feeling awkward again for the first time in years.

"Hello."

"I hope you don't mind," he said, glancing from her to the painting.

"Not at all. I'm honored you'd remember that night." She looked more closely at the painting. "I still have that formal."

He looked at her while she gazed at the painting. He was now three or four inches taller than she. She was still beautiful, but he was a little disappointed that she'd lost much of her country charm. She wore more makeup now than when he'd known her. From what she was wearing—a light orange dress—he realized she was very much aware of what she looked good in. He could see she spent much more time on herself than she had in high school. Somewhere along the way she must have discovered how beautiful she could be if she put forth a little effort.

Kade wondered what it was like for Brenda at BYU. She was someone you couldn't help but notice even if you only passed her on a sidewalk between classes. And yet, for all her beauty, she wasn't the same as she'd been in high school, and for some reason that disappointed him.

She turned to look at him. "I see you finally got those contact lenses you wanted so much."

He blushed, not because he was wearing contacts, but because he realized she was thinking the same thing about him, that he'd changed.

"Yes."

"You were right to get them. You have nice eyes."

He smiled. " 'The better to see you with, my dear.' "

She turned back to the painting. "It's a wonderful painting," she said.

"I've done a couple more of you."

"I'd love to see them."

"Sometime when I come down here, I'll bring them along."

"Do you come down here often?" she asked.

"Yes," he lied.

"Call me up when you get into town the next time," she said. "Maybe we can go practice kicking field goals."

It struck a resonant chord. He realized that even

though they were now both much different from before, their memories, like deep roots, were the same.

"How're your folks?" he asked.

"They're fine. My dad really likes what he's doing. I know he'd like to see you again." She paused. "Do you ski?"

"Not really."

"Show up in Vail sometime, and my dad and I'll teach you."

"Sounds like a good deal."

She hesitated, then said, "Actually, if you're really interested, I could teach you here in Utah."

"I'd like that." He smiled. "Seems like you're always teaching me things, doesn't it?"

"I'm sure there're plenty of things you could teach me. I'd really like to hear about your mission."

Suddenly he realized that two coeds were standing next to them, not looking at his painting, but staring at him and Brenda.

"Is there someplace we can go and be alone?"

"Wow," one of the girls said, "we've got fireworks here, don't we!"

He tried to ignore the remark but felt his face getting red. "Just someplace where we can talk and maybe get something to drink."

Brenda nodded. "I know just the place. It's in the Wilkinson Center. Can you leave now?"

"Yes."

The faculty member in charge of the exhibit saw them leaving. "We'd prefer that you stay by your painting until nine o'clock."

"We won't be long."

They walked out into the cold winter night. It was snowing.

"Let's see," he said. "I was younger than you the night of the prom, wasn't I?"

"And you're not now?" she teased.

"Not anymore. Now we're the same age."

She nodded. "I guess I feel that way too."

He reached out and held her hand.

"Kade, do you think we might become good friends again?"

"I hope so."

"Me too. I've really missed having a friend like you."

"I've missed it too."

They got their drinks and then returned to the exhibit until it closed. He drove her home. She invited him in, and he met her roommates. They sat around the kitchen table and talked until midnight. She invited him to come for breakfast in the morning before he headed back to Ricks.

After he returned to the guest housing the university had arranged for him, even though it was late, he took out a piece of paper and drew yet another picture of Brenda.

It felt good to be home again.